Strange Stories
Day

Various

Alpha Editions

This edition published in 2024

ISBN : 9789362994455

Design and Setting By
Alpha Editions
www.alphaedis.com
Email - info@alphaedis.com

As per information held with us this book is in Public Domain.
This book is a reproduction of an important historical work. Alpha Editions uses the best technology to reproduce historical work in the same manner it was first published to preserve its original nature. Any marks or number seen are left intentionally to preserve its true form.

Contents

INTRODUCTION ....- 1 -

I THE CROWNING OF POWHATAN
Adventures in Early Indian History ....- 2 -

II CORNELIS LABDEN'S LEAP A Legend
of 1645 Retold..- 6 -

III TOMMY TEN-CANOES A Tale of King
Philip's Scout ....- 12 -

IV JONATHAN'S ESCAPE A Young Hero
of Hadley who Fought at Turner's Falls in
1676..- 19 -

V THE CROWN OF AN AMERICAN
QUEEN In the Days of Bacon's Rebellion
in Virginia ....- 23 -

VI HOW A BLACKSMITH'S BOY
BECAME A KNIGHT The Treasure-hunt of
William Phipps in the late Seventeenth
Century...- 26 -

VII THE GIRL CAPTAIN OF CASTLE
DANGEROUS How Three Children Fought
the Iroquois in 1692 ....- 31 -

VIII HOW MARC WAS MADE CAPTAIN
A Rescue from the "Lords of the Woods" in
1695..- 35 -

IX CAPTAIN KIDD An Overrated Pirate .... - 42 -

X HOWARD THE BUCCANEER A
Captain of Many Ships .... - 49 -

XI TEW, OF RHODE ISLAND A Fighter
from the Seas .... - 56 -

XII THE VROUW VAN TWINKLE'S
KRULLERS A Story of Old New York .... - 65 -

XIII THE SIGN OF THE SERPENT A
Story of Louisiana in the Early Eighteenth
Century .... - 74 -

XIV A DRUMMER OF WARBURTON'S
How a Boy Held Fort George at Cape
Canso, in 1757 .... - 81 -

XV ROGERS' RANGERS The Famous
New Hampshire Scouts of the Old French
War .... - 88 -

XVI THE PLOT OF PONTIAC How
Detroit was Saved in 1763 .... - 92 -

INTRODUCTION

These pictures of Colonial life and adventure make up a panorama which extends from Powhatan and John Smith, in the days of the Jamestown colony, to Pontiac's attempt upon Detroit in the period which preceded the Revolution. Here one may read stories which are strange indeed, of King Philip's War in New England, of a Dutch hero's exploit on the shores of Long Island Sound, of conflicts with the fierce Iroquois in the North, of a young New Englander's successful treasure-hunt, and of famous or infamous pirates of Colonial times. They carry the reader from a boy's defence of Fort George in Nova Scotia to battle against the Natchez at an advance post of the Louisiana colony. For the most part these thrilling tales are in theform of fiction, but it is fiction based upon historical incidents. The imaginative stories, and others which are historical narratives, will, it is believed, illustrate many unfamiliar dramas in Colonial life, and will help to give a clearer view of the men and boys who fought and endured to clear the way for us upon this continent.

I
THE CROWNING OF POWHATAN
ADVENTURES IN EARLY INDIAN HISTORY

The first European visitors to the shores of North America met with a most friendly reception from the natives. Powhatan, the Indian Emperor of Virginia, who ruled in savage state over twenty-six Indian nations, on more than one occasion kept the Virginia colonists from starvation by sending them corn when they were almost famished. To retain his good-will a crown was sent over from England, and the Indian monarch was crowned with as much ceremony as possible. A present from King James of a basin and ewer, a bed, and some clothes was also brought to Jamestown, but Powhatan refused to go there to receive it.

"I also am a King, and gifts should be brought to me," said the proud monarch of the Virginia woods. They were accordingly taken to him by the colonists.

The coronation was "a sad trouble," wrote Captain John Smith, but it had its laughable side also, as we shall see. Custom required that the Indian ruler should kneel. Only by bearing their whole weight upon his shoulders could the English upon whom this duty devolved bring the chief from an upright position into one suitable to the occasion. By main force he was made to kneel.

The firing of a pistol as a signal for a volley from the boats in honor of the event startled his copper-colored Majesty. Supposing himself betrayed, Powhatan at once struck a defensive attitude, but was soon reassured. The absurdity of the whole affair reached its climax when Powhatan gave to the representatives of his royal brother in England his old moccasins, the deerskin he used as a blanket, and a few bushels of corn in the ear.

On the New England coast the anger of the natives had been aroused by the conduct of visiting sailors, who would persuade them to come on board their ships, and then carry them off and sell them into slavery.

One of these natives, named Epanow, "an Indian of goodly stature, strong, and well proportioned," after being exhibited in London as a curiosity, came into the service of Sir Ferdinand Gorges, Governor of Plymouth. This gentleman was much interested in New England, and was about fitting out a ship for a voyage to this country.

The Indian soon found out that gold was the great object of the Englishman's worship, and he was cunning enough to take advantage of the fact. He assured Sir Ferdinand that in a certain place in his own country gold was to be had in abundance. The Englishman believed him, and Epanow sailed in Gorges's vessel to point out the whereabouts of the supposed gold-mine.

When the ship entered the harbor many of the natives came on board. Epanow arranged with them a plan of escape, which was successfully carried out the next morning.

At the appointed time twenty canoes full of armed Indians came to within a short distance of the ship. The captain invited them to come on board. Epanow had been clothed in long garments, that he might the more easily be laid hold of in case he attempted to escape, and he was also closely guarded by three of Gorges's kinsmen.

The critical moment arrived. Epanow suddenly freed himself from his guards, and springing over the vessel's side, succeeded in reaching his countrymen in safety, though many shots were fired after him by the English.

In this affair the European was completely outwitted by the ignorant savage. Gorges was bitterly disappointed. Writing of it he says, "And thus were my hopes of that particular voyage made void and frustrate." And thus, we may add, the first gold-hunting expedition to the coast of Maine "ended in smoke"—from the Englishmen's guns.

For many years after the landing of the Pilgrims at Plymouth the relations of the English with the Massachusetts Indians were peaceful. Only once was there any attempt to disturb them. To try the mettle of the colonists, Canonicus, the powerful Narragansett chief, sent them by a messenger a bundle of arrows wrapped in the skin of a snake—a challenge to fight. Governor Bradford returned the skin filled with powder and shot, with the message that if they had rather have war than peace they might begin when they pleased, he was ready for them. This prompt defiance impressed the chief. He would not receive the skin, and wisely concluded to keep the peace.

What is known as King Philip's War broke out in 1675. Though it lasted but little over a year, it was terribly destructive, and it carried misery to many a hearth-stone.

Philip of Pokanoket, the chief of the Wampanoags, had for years been suspected of plotting against the English. He had resisted all their efforts to convert his people to Christianity, and had told the venerable apostle Eliot himself that he cared no more for the white man's religion than for the buttons on his (Eliot's) coat. On another occasion he refused to make a treaty with the Governor of Massachusetts, sending him this answer:

"Your Governor is but a subject of King Charles of England. I shall not treat with a subject. I shall treat of peace only with the King, my brother. When he comes, I am ready."

On the morning of April 10, 1671, the meeting-house on Taunton Green presented a scene of extraordinary interest. Seated on the benches upon one side of the house were Philip and his warriors, and on the other side were the white men. Both parties were equipped for battle. The Indians looked as formidable as possible in their war-paint, their hair "trimmed up in comb fashion," with their long bows and quivers of arrows, and here and there a gun in the hands of those best skilled in its use. The English wore the costume of Cromwell, with broad-brimmed hats, cuirasses, long swords, and unwieldly guns. Each party looked at the other with unconcealed hatred.

The result of this conference was that the Indians agreed to give up all their guns, and Philip, upon his part, also promised to send a yearly tribute of five wolves' heads—"If he could get them."

As the Indians had almost forgotten how to use their old weapons, the taking of their fire-arms away was a serious grievance. Other causes of enmity arose, and at last the war begun, which in its course caused the destruction of thirteen towns and hundreds of valuable lives.

Philip was joined by the Nipmucks, as the Indians of the interior were called, and by the Narragansetts, whose stronghold was captured in the winter of 1675-76. Here seven hundred of this hapless tribe perished by fire or the sword. The death of Philip, in August, 1676, ended the war. Many of the Indians fled to the west, and a large number died in slavery in the West Indies. The power of the Indians of southern New England was broken forever.

Captain Benjamin Church, a prominent actor in this war, was the most celebrated Indian fighter of his day. One of his most remarkable feats was the capture of Annawan, Philip's chief captain. Annawan often said that he would never be taken by the English.

Informed by a captured Indian where Annawan lay, Church, with only one other Englishman and a few friendly Indians, succeeded in gaining the rear of the Indian camp.

The approach to this secluded spot was extremely difficult. It was nearly dark when they reached it, and the Indians were preparing their evening meal. A little apart from the others, and within easy reach of the guns of the party, the chief and his son were reclining on the ground. An old squaw was pounding corn in a mortar, the noise of which prevented the discovery of Church's approach, as he and his companions cautiously lowered themselves from rock to rock. They were preceded by an old Indian and his daughter, whom they had captured, and who, with their baskets at their backs, aided in concealing their approach.

By these skilful tactics Church succeeded in placing himself between the chief and the guns, seeing which, Annawan suddenly started up with the cry, "Howoh!" ("I am taken.") Perceiving that he was surrounded, he made no attempt to escape.

After securing the arms, Church sent his Indian scouts among Annawan's men to tell them that their chief was captured, and that Church with his great army had entrapped them, and would cut them to pieces unless they surrendered. This they accordingly did, and, on the promise of kind treatment, gave up all their arms. This well-executed surprise was the closing event of King Philip's War.

II
CORNELIS LABDEN'S LEAP
A LEGEND OF 1645 RETOLD

The scene was only thirty miles from New York, on the shores of Long Island Sound. At the time of which we write it was a sweep of dense forest.

Outside of the block-house, built where the Myanos River enters a bay of the Sound, one September day in 1645 walked two elderly men, grizzled of beard and soldierly in bearing. Broadswords swung from their cross-belts and huge pistolets were stuck in their girdles. These were famous fighting men in New England history, Daniel Patrick and John Underhill. Bred to camps, they had chafed under Puritan laws, and had finally deserted the older settlements. Indeed, Captain Patrick had been the leader of the little colony which had made this beautiful place its home.

"I tell thee, John, I trust not the savage any longer. Ponus hath been as surly as a bear with a sore head of late. I fear the Sagamore plots evil."

"Belike you are right, good Captain," said Underhill, "and we must match craft with craft."

"Rumor hath it, too," said Captain Patrick, with growing trouble on his face, "that strange runners have been back and forth during the month at the Sinoway village. We cannot look to our English friends for help, since we signed the pact with his Excellency Governor Kieft, accepting the rule of New Netherland. If an outbreak occurs, it must be from the Manhattans that relief will come. But look! there rides Dutch Cornelis with a bale of peltries to his crupper."

Among a few Dutch who mingled with the English of the settlement was Cornelis Labden, a bold hunter and trapper, who, unlike the rest of the colonists, got his livelihood by the fur-trade. He sold his pelts at the Dutch trading-post about seven miles west, just over the line which now separates New York from Connecticut. Thither he was riding when accosted by the two captains. Cornelis was noted for his daring and skill in woodcraft, and had always lived on specially friendly terms with the Indians, as was, indeed, his interest. His log house was built on the brow of a great precipice of beetling rock one hundred feet or more in height, in the heart of a gloomy forest two miles from the outskirts of the settlement. The spot is still known as Labden's Rock, and the writer has shot many a squirrel there in woods still solemn with deepest shadow. Here Cornelis lived with his English wife and two children, Hans and Anneke.

"Well met, Cornelis," said Patrick. "We were holding counsel concerning our Indian neighbors. What think you of their peaceful purpose?"

The Dutchman shook his head. He was a man of few words. "Der outlook ist pad, Cabdain. Dot yoong Gief Owenoke say to me toder day, 'Cornelis, Indian's friend, bedder go 'way. Indian very angry at bale-faces.' Owenoke's vader, Ponus, means misgief. But no tanger dill der snow vlies. Der Indians, if dey addack, waid dill grops all in."

"You are bound, I suppose, to Byram Fort with your peltries. Tarry awhile, and carry me a letter for the Governor. I will write it forthwith." Captain Patrick disappeared in the block-house, and wrote to the Dutch Governor as follows:

"To his Excellency, Wilhelm Kieft, Governor-General of New Netherland at New Amsterdam, greeting:

"This in haste:—Whereas it cometh to me with some surety that the savages on our border plot an early outbreak, I would urge that a company of musketeers be sent to the trading-post at Byram to protect the outlying country. Thence sure help may reach this settlement. Once the savages break loose they will ravage the region for many miles with torch and tomahawk. I would entreat your Excellency to act right speedily in this affair. Cornelis Labden, who is well skilled in Indian matters, bears this letter.

"Daniel Patrick."

It will be seen by this that Captain Patrick did not share the confidence of Cornelis. But all the people were very busy afield at that time gathering their crops, and they were loath to think that danger was pressing. The women and children, however, were gathered every night in the block-house. It may be that this measure of care on the part of the settlers quickened the action of the Indians in the fear that their purpose had been discovered. Within three days the outbreak came. The forest was glowing with all the rich hues of autumn, when through its arches burst at different points bands of naked warriors, painted with as many colors as the leaves themselves, and yelling their shrill war-whoops. Every colonist amid the yellowing corn-stalks of the fields had his firelock close at hand. They all skirmished back through this cover and across the rye and buckwheat stubble towards the block-house, firing and loading as they ran. Yet several fell under the cloud of arrows before the fugitives reached the little fort. The two captains, each with a party of men, charged the savages fiercely on either flank as they leaped into the open, and drove them back with heavy loss. The settlers then withdrew behind the palisades, awaiting attack.

The red besiegers, having exhausted their arts of attack and met with heavy loss, for musket-balls told with terrible effect against flint arrows, determined to starve out the little garrison. It was on the morning of the third day that a rider galloped furiously from the west to the bank of the Myanos, where the log bridge had been destroyed by the Indians. Dutch Cornelis had ridden daringly through the midst of them. A band of howling braves swarmed almost at his horse's tail. He leaped his beast into the river amid the whizzing arrows, several of which stung both steed and rider sharply. Captain Underhill, with a score of colonists, sallied out from the palisades, driving the redskins from their front and opening a heavy fire on those lining the opposite bank. Under cover of this Cornelis landed safely. He had been sent on from Byram to New Amsterdam with Patrick's letter, and it was only by hard spurring that he had made such speed in return. He brought the good news that even then a company of Dutch musketeers was on the march.

The women and children trooped out of the block-house to hear the tidings. Cornelis cast his eyes over them with agony stamped on his usually stolid face.

"Mein vrouw! mein gildren!" the Dutchman groaned. "What for you leave dem to de mercy of de savage?" with a look of fierce reproach at the two English captains.

"MEIN VROUW! MEIN GILDREN!" THE DUTCHMAN GROANED

"Nay! nay! Cornelis, blame us not," they answered, almost in a breath. "We were sharp beset. 'Twas not easy to gather in all the outlying people in season. There be others as well not saved in the block. The savage, too, is far more friendly to you than to us English. There's right good hope that at the worst the lost are but captives."

This cold comfort seemed to madden the bereaved man. Muttering to himself in his own tongue, and darting wild looks around, as if his brain were turned and he were about to run amuck, he suddenly sprang on his horse, which panted there, fagged and dripping.

"Oben der gate!" he shouted, in a tone so commanding that, though several tried to seize his horse's head by the bit, fearing some act of desperate folly, others unbarred the entrance. Cornelis dashed through as swiftly as an Indian arrow. Two miles of clearing and forest lay between him and his cabin. The way was thick with savages thirsting for blood. Cornelis spurred on, numb to all sense of danger. The smoke even yet curled from the embers of smouldering homesteads at every turn. But he saw only one house in his mind's eye—that was a cabin perched in the midst of a clearing on top of a great rock, with flames bursting from its roof; he heard but one sound—the shrieking of wife and children in their last peril.

Perhaps it was the wild gestures of the rider, signalling as if to unseen beings, the motions of a maniac, which barred any pursuit at the outset, for the American Indian as well as the Mohammedan of the East fancies the madman under the protection of God; perhaps it was that many of the savages felt more kindly to Cornelis than to other whites. It was not till he neared the base of the precipice, on the crest of which he had built his home, that he saw six Indians on his track, leaping at a pace which outran the strides of his weary horse.

The Dutchman turned in his saddle, and his unerring aim dropped one of the pursuers; then he urged his way amid the gloom of the great trees up the hill. When he gained the clearing at the top he saw what had once been his happy home, now only a pile of cold ashes and half-charred logs. He had no time to search if by chance there might yet remain some ghastly relic of those he had loved and lost. The red men were upon him, running as fleetly as stag-hounds, for now they were on the level.

They were sure of their prey. A triumphant whoop rang out. Tomahawks whizzed through the air, one of them striking Cornelis in the shoulder, as the savages pressed on at top speed. The white man laughed loud and long with a laughter that filled the forest with shrill echoes, and motioning to them as if he were their leader, leaped his horse from the top of the terrible rock, crashing through the branches of trees down, down a hundred feet. The human hounds so hot in the chase were going with a rush which could not be stayed, and they too plunged to death in the pathway of their victim. Cornelis escaped with broken limbs, though his horse was killed, and all the Indians perished but one, who saved himself by clutching at the limb of a tree. He fled and carried the story to his tribe.

With the coming of the Dutch soldiers the settlers were strong enough to scatter their assailants. But most of the colonists, discouraged, drifted away to the New Netherlands or to the more easterly settlements. It was not till two years later that a force of Dutch and English stormed the Sinoway village and crushed the power of the tribe, after which the town was successfully settled.

Ten years have passed. The skill and toil of the whites have swept away the scars of Indian warfare. Pleasant homes rise amid smiling fields of maize and rye. One summer day, Cornelis Labden, a helpless cripple and almost half-witted, sat on the porch of Captain Underhill's house, smoking his long Dutch pipe and looking at the shining waters of the Sound. Here or in the good Captain's hearth-corner he would doze and mumble all day long summer and winter. An Indian youth, nearly grown, walked up the lane and stood before this poor wreck of a man. Cornelis shut his eyes, and waved him off as if to drive away some thought that troubled his weak brain.

"Lapten, me find Lapten," said the Indian, whose blue eyes and brown hair were queerly amiss with the copper skin, the breech-clout, and the moccasins of the savage.

The sound of the voice stirred Cornelis strangely, and as if by some instinct he spoke in Dutch. The lad listened eagerly, for the words seemed to be half known to him, and he repeated them. Cornelis watched him with an intent look, like the gaze of one just awakened from a long sleep. He trembled, and for the first time in years intelligence burned in his eyes. Without another word he led the Indian lad within and began to rub the skin of his face with soap and water, and in a few moments the clear white was shown. While he was thus engaged over the unresisting youth, Captain Underhill entered.

"Cabdain, Cabdain," said Cornelis, with a shaking voice, "mein Hans ist goom back. Done ye know yer old vader, leedle Hans? Vare ist Anneke?" And he threw his arms with a passion of sobs about the lad's neck. This opened the gates of memory for father and son, and the identity was soon made clear. In recovering his son, Dutch Cornelis had also regained his reason.

By gradual questioning, the facts were fully obtained as the half-forgotten language of childhood came back. Hans and Anneke had been carried off by strange Indians of the more northern tribes, who had sent warriors to join in the Sinoway attack.

The children had been separated, and Anneke was lost forever. As Hans grew up, forgetting much, he still remembered his father's name and his white blood. He had finally escaped from his adopted tribe, and worked his way by a strange series of accidents and guesses back to the place of his birth. Such, in the main, is the legend of Labden's Rock.

III
TOMMY TEN-CANOES
A TALE OF KING PHILIP'S SCOUT

There once lived in New York an Indian warrior by the name of Peter Twenty-Canoes. Tommy Ten-Canoes lived in New England, at Pokanoket, near Mount Hope, on an arm of the Mount Hope Bay.

He was not a warrior, but a runner; not a great naval hero, as his picturesque name might suggest, but a news agent, as it were; he used his nimble feet and his ten canoes to bear messages to the Indians of the villages of Pokanoket and to the Narragansetts, and, it may be, to other friendly tribes.

Pokanoket? You may have read Irving's sketch of Philip of Pokanoket, but we doubt if you have in mind any clear idea of this beautiful region, from whose clustering wigwams the curling smoke once rose among the giant oaks along the many waterways. The former site of Pokanoket is now covered by Bristol and Warren (Rhode Island) and Swansea (Massachusetts). It is a place of bays and rivers, which were once rich fishing-grounds; of shores full of shells and shellfish; of cool springs and wild-grape vines; of bowery hills; and of meadows that were once yellow with maize.

Tommy Ten-Canoes was a great man in his day. As a news agent in peace he was held in high honor, but as a scout in war and a runner for the great chiefs he became a heroic figure. There were great osprey's nests all about the shores of old Pokanoket on the ancient decayed trees, and Tommy made a crown of osprey feathers, and crowned himself, with the approval of the great Indian chiefs.

Once when swimming with this crown of feathers on his head, he had been shot at by an Englishman, who thought him some new and remarkable bird. But while his crown was shattered, it was not the crown of his head. He was very careful of both his crowns after that alarming event.

Tommy Ten-Canoes was a brave man. He was ready to face any ordinary danger for his old chief Massasoit, and for that chief's two sons, Wamsutta (Alexander) and Pomebacen (Philip). He would cross the Mount Hope or the Narragansett bay in tempestuous weather. He used to convey the beautiful Queen Weetamoc from Pocassett to Mount Hope to attend Philip's war-dances under the summer moons, and when the old Indian war began he offered his two swift legs and all of his ten canoes to the service of his chief.

"Nipanset"—for this was his Indian name—"Nipanset's bosom is his chief's, and it knows not fear. Nipanset fears not the storm or the foe, or the gun of the pale-face. Call, call, O ye chiefs; in the hour of danger call for Nipanset. Nipanset fears not death."

So Tommy Ten-Canoes boasted at the great council under the moss-covered cliff at Mount Hope.

He was honest; but there was one thing that Nipanset, or Tommy Ten-Canoes, did fear. It was enchantment. He would have faced torture or death without a word, but everything mysterious filled him with terror. If he had thought that a bush contained a hidden enemy and flintlock, he would have been very brave; but had he thought that the same bush was stirred by a spirit, or was enchanted, he would have run.

Tommy Ten-Canoes had been friendly to the white people who had settled in Pokanoket. There was a family by the name of Brown, who lived on Cole's River, that he especially liked, and he became a companion of one of the sons named James. The two were so often together that the people used to speak of those who were very intimate as being "as thick as little James Brown and old Tommy Ten-Canoes," or rather as "Jemmie Brown" and our young hero of the many birch boats.

The two hunted and fished together; they made long journeys together; in fact, they did everything in common, except work. Tommy did not work, at least in the field, while James did at times, when he was not with Tommy.

When the Indian war began, King Philip sent word to the Brown family, and also to the Cole family, who lived near them, both of whom had treated him justly and generously, that he would do all in his power to protect them, but that he might not be able to restrain his braves.

Tommy Ten-Canoes brought a like friendly message to Jemmie Brown.

"I will always be true to you," he said; "true as the north wind to the river, the west wind to the sea, and the south wind to the flowers. Nipanset's heart is true to his friends. Our hearts will see each other again."

The Indian torch swept the settlements. One of the bravest scouts in these dark scenes was Tommy Ten-Canoes. He flew from place to place like the wind, carrying news and spying out the enemy.

Tommy grew proud over his title of "Ten-Canoes." He felt like ten Tommies. He wore his crown of osprey feathers like a royal king. His ten canoes ferried the painted Indians at night, and carried the chiefs hither and thither.

There was a grizzly old Boston Captain, who had done hard service on the sea, named Moseley. He wore a wig, a thing that the Indians had never seen, and of whose use they knew nothing at all.

Tommy Ten-Canoes had never feared the white man nor the latter's death-dealing weapons. He had never retreated; he had always been found in front of the stealthy bands as they pursued the forest trails. But his courage was at last put to a test of which he had never dreamed.

Old Captain Moseley had led a company of trained soldiers against the Indians from Boston. Tommy Ten-Canoes had discovered the movement, and had prepared the Indians to meet it. Captain Moseley's company, which consisted of one hundred men, had first marched to a place called Myles Bridge in Swansea. Here was a garrison house in which lived Rev. John Myles. The church was called Baptist, but people of all faiths were welcome to it; among the latter, Marinus Willett, who afterwards became the first Mayor of New York. It was the first church of the kind in Massachusetts, and it still exists in Swansea.

Over the glimmering waterways walled with dark oak woods came Tommy Ten-Canoes, with five of his famous boats, and landed at a place near the thrifty Baptist colony, so that his little navy might be at the ready service of Philip. It was the last days of June. There had been an eclipse of the moon on the night that Tommy Ten-Canoes had glided up the Sowans River towards Myles Bridge. He thought the eclipse was meant for him and his little boats, and he was a very proud and happy man.

"The moon went out in the clear sky when we left the bay," said he; "so shall our enemies be extinguished. The moon shone again on the calm river. For whom did the moon shine again? For Nipanset."

Poor Tommy Ten-Canoes! He was not the first hero of modern times who has thought that the moon and stars were made for him and shone for him on special occasions.

In old Captain Moseley's company was a Jamaica pilot who had visited Pokanoket and been presented to Tommy, and told that the latter was a very renowned Indian.

"What are you?" asked the Pilot.

"I am Tommy One-Canoe."

"Ah!"

"I am Tommy Two-Canoes."

"Indeed! Ah!"

"I am Tommy Three-Canoes."

"Oh! Ah! Indeed!"

"I am Tommy Four-Canoes, and I am Tommy Five-Canoes, and I am Tommy Six-Canoes, and I am Tommy TEN-Canoes."

"Well, Tommy Ten-Canoes," said the Pilot, "don't you ever get into any trouble with the white people, because you might find yourself merely Tommy No-Canoes."

Tommy was offended at this. He had no fears of such a fall from power, however.

The old Jamaica pilot had taken a boat and drifted down the Sowans River one long June day, when he chanced to discover Tommy and his five canoes. The canoes were hauled up on the shore under the cool trees which overshadowed the water. The Pilot, who had with him three men, rowed boldly to the shore and surprised Tommy Ten-Canoes, who had gone into the wood, leaving his weapons in one of his canoes.

The Pilot seized the canoe with the weapons and drew it from the shore.

Tommy Ten-Canoes beheld the movement with astonishment. He called to the old Pilot, "I am Tommy Ten-Canoes!"

"No, no," answered the Pilot. "You are Tommy Nine-Canoes."

Presently the Pilot drew from the shore another canoe. Tommy called again:

"Don't you know me? I am—"

"Tommy Eight-Canoes," said the Pilot.

Another boat was removed in like manner, and the Pilot shouted, "And now you are Tommy Seven-Canoes." Another, and the Pilot called again, "Now you are Tommy Six-Canoes." Another. "Good-bye, Tommy Five-Canoes," said the Pilot, and he and his men drew all of the light canoes after them up the river.

"GOOD-BYE, TOMMY FIVE-CANOES"

Xerxes at Salamis could hardly have felt more crushed in heart than Tommy Ten-Canoes. But hope revived; he was Tommy Five-Canoes still. He was not quite so sure now, however, that the moon on that still June night had been eclipsed expressly for him.

The scene of the war now changed to the western border, as the towns of Hadley and Deerfield were called, for these towns in that day were the "great west," as afterwards was the Ohio Reserve. Tommy having lost five of his canoes, now used his swift feet as a messenger. He still had hopes of doing great deeds, else why had the moon been eclipsed on that beautiful June night?

But an event followed the loss of his five canoes that quite changed his opinion. As a messenger or runner he had hurried to the scene of the brutal conflicts on the border, and had there discovered that Captain Moseley, the old Jamaica pirate, was subject to some spell of enchantment; that he had two heads.

"Ugh! ugh! him no good!" said one of the Indians to Tommy; "he take off his head and put him in his pocket. It is no use to fight him. Spell set on him—enchanted."

Tommy Ten-Canoes' fear of the man with two heads, one of which he sometimes took off and put in his pocket, spread among the Indians. One day in a skirmish Tommy saw Moseley take off one of his enchanted heads and hang it on a blueberry bush. Other Indians saw it. "No scalp him," said they. "Run!" And run they did, not from the open foe, but from the supposed head on the bush. Moseley did not dream at the time that it was his wig that had given him the victory.

Across the Mount Hope Bay, among the sunny headlands of Pocassett, there was an immense cedar swamp, cool and dark, and in summer full of fire-flies. Tommy Ten-Canoes called it the swamp of the fire-flies. It was directly opposite Pokanoket, across the placid water. A band of Indians gathered there, and covered their bodies with bushes, so that they might not be discovered on the shore.

One moonlight night in September Tommy went to visit these masked Indians in four of his canoes. He rowed one of his canoes, and three squaws the others. On reaching the fire-fly cedar swamp the party met the masked Indians, and late at night retired to rest, the three Indian squaws sleeping on the shore under their three canoes.

Captain Moseley had sent the old Jamaica pilot to try to discover the hiding-place of this mysterious band of Indians. The Pilot had seen the four canoes crossing the bay from Pokanoket under the low September moon, and had hurried with a dozen men to the place of landing. He surprised the party early the next morning, when they were disarmed and asleep.

The crack of his musket rang out in the clear air over the bay. A naked Indian was seen to leap up.

"Stop! I am Tommy Ten-Canoes."

"No, Tommy Five-Canoes," answered the Pilot; "and now you are only Tommy Four-Canoes." Saying which, the Pilot seized the sixth canoe.

A shriek followed; another, and another. Three canoes hidden in the river-weeds were overturned, and three Indian squaws were seen running into the dark swamp.

"And now you are Tommy Three-Canoes," said the Pilot, seizing the seventh canoe. "And now Tommy Two-Canoes," seizing the eighth.

"And only Tommy One-Canoe," taking possession of the ninth canoe. "And now you are Tommy No-Canoes, as I told you you would be if you went to war," said the Pilot, taking according to this odd reckoning the Indian's last canoe.

But Tommy had one canoe left, notwithstanding the dark Pilot had taken his tenth. He was glad that it was not here. It would have been his eleventh canoe, although he had but ten. He knew that the Pilot was one of Moseley's men, the Captain who put his head at times in his pocket or hung it upon a bush. Poor Tommy Ten-Canoes! He uttered a shriek, like the fugitive squaws, and fled.

"Don't shoot at him," said the old Pilot to his men. "I have taken from him all of his ten canoes; let him go."

Tommy had not a mathematical mind or education, but he knew that somehow he had no eleventh canoe, and that one of his ten canoes yet remained. And even the old Pilot must have at last seen that his count of ten was only nine. Tommy fled to a point on the Titicut River at which he could swim across, and then made his solitary way back to the shores of Pokanoket and to his remaining canoe, which did not belong to mathematics.

One morning late in September Tommy Ten-Canoes turned his solitary canoe towards Cole's River, near which lived his boy friend, James Brown. He paddled slowly, and late in the dreamy afternoon reached the shore opposite the Brown farm. He landed and tied his one canoe to Jemmie Brown's boat, in which the two had spent many happy hours before the war.

The canoe was found there the next day; but Tommy Ten-Canoes? He was never seen again; he probably sought a grave in the waters of the bay.

But he had fulfilled his promise. He had been true in his heart as "the north wind to the river, the west wind to the sea, and the south wind to the flowers."

IV
JONATHAN'S ESCAPE
A YOUNG HERO OF HADLEY WHO FOUGHT AT TURNER'S FALLS IN 1676

Though the Indians of New England were for many years vastly superior in numbers to the white men, they were never wholly united, and their cowardice and lack of discipline were weaknesses for which their treachery and deceit could not compensate. The long conflict between the races culminated in 1675 in King Philip's War, when the wily Wampanoag sachem succeeded in forming a confederation, embracing nearly all the New England tribes, for a final desperate struggle.

It seemed for a time as though the combination might succeed. At the end of the summer the scattered settlements, and especially those along the Connecticut River, which formed the outposts of the colonies, were panic-stricken. Everywhere the savage allies had been victorious. A dozen towns had been attacked and burned, bands of soldiers had been cut off, and isolated murders without number had been committed. Prowling bands of Indians lurked about the stockaded towns, driving off cattle and rendering impossible the cultivation of the fields, so that the settlers were called upon to face starvation as well as the scalping-knife and tomahawk.

There was no meeting the Indians face to face, except by surprise. They fought from ambush, or by sudden assault on unprotected points, and would be gone before troops could be brought to the scene. The white men were unable to follow them without Indian allies, and they were slow to adapt themselves to the Indian mode of fighting. Flushed by their success, the confederates became overconfident, and grew to despise their clumsy opponents. In the spring of 1676 more than five thousand of them were encamped on the Connecticut River, twenty miles north of Hadley. Here they planted their corn and squashes, and amused themselves with councils, ceremonies, and feasts, boasting of what they had done and what they would do. They judged the white men by themselves, and did not suspect the iron courage and stubborn determination that were urging the people in the towns below them "to be out against the enemy." On the night of May 18th they indulged in a great feast, and after it was over, slept soundly in their bark lodges, all but the wary Philip, who, scenting danger, had withdrawn across the river.

On that same evening about two hundred and fifty men and boys gathered in Hadley street. Of this number fifty-six were soldiers from the garrisons of Hadley, Northampton, Springfield, Hatfield, and Westfield. The rest were volunteers, among whom was Jonathan Wells, of Hadley, sixteen years old, whose adventures and miraculous escape have been preserved.

The party was under the command of Captain William Turner, and the expedition which it was about to undertake was inspired by a daring amounting to rashness. The plan was to attack the Indian camp, which contained four times their number of well-armed braves. Defeat meant death, or captivity and torture worse than death. The march began after nightfall so as not to attract the attention of the Indian scouts, and the little band made its way safely through swamps and forests, past the Indian outposts, and at daybreak arrived in the neighborhood of the camp. Here the horses were left under a small guard among the trees, while the men crept forward to the lodges of the enemy.

The surprise was complete. The panic-stricken savages, crying that the dreaded Mohawks were upon them, were shot down by scores, or, plunging into the river, were swept over the falls which now bear Captain Turner's name. The backbone of Philip's conspiracy was broken, and he himself was driven to begin soon afterwards the hunted wanderings which were to end in the fatal morass.

But the attacking party, though victorious, was not yet out of danger. It was still heavily outnumbered by the surviving Indians. While the soldiers were destroying arms, ammunition, and food, or scattered in pursuit of the fleeing enemy, the warriors rallied, and opened fire upon them from under cover of the trees. Captain Turner became alarmed and ordered a retreat. The main body hastily mounted and plunged into the forest, seeking to shake off the cloud of savages who hung upon their flanks like a swarm of angry bees.

Young Jonathan was with a detachment of about twenty who were some distance up the river when the retreat began. They ran back to the horses and found their comrades gone. The Indians pressed upon them in numbers they could not hope to withstand. It was every man for himself. In the confusion the boy kept his wits about him, and managed to find his horse. As he plunged forward under the branches three Indians levelled their pieces and fired. One shot passed through his hair, another struck his horse, and the third entered his thigh, splintering the bone where it had been broken by a cart-wheel and never properly healed. He reeled, and would have fallen had he not clutched the mane of his horse. The Indians, seeing that he was wounded, pursued him, but he pointed his gun at them, and held them at bay until he was out of their reach. As he galloped on he heard a cry for help, and reining in his horse, regardless of the danger which encompassed him, found Stephen Belding, a boy of his own age, lying sorely wounded on the ground. He managed to pull him up behind, and they rode double until they overtook the party in advance. This brave act saved Belding's life.

The retreat had become a rout. All was panic and dismay; but Jonathan was unwilling to desert the comrades left behind. He sought out Captain Turner, and begged him to halt and turn back to their relief. "It is better to save some than to lose all," was the Captain's answer. The confusion increased, and to add to it the guides became bewildered and lost their way. "If you love your lives, follow me!" cried one. "If you would see your homes again! follow me," shouted another, and the party was soon split up into small bands. The one with which Jonathan found himself became entangled in a swamp, where it was once more attacked by the Indians. He escaped again, with ten others, who, finding that his horse was going lame from his wound, and that he himself was weak from loss of blood, left him with another wounded man and rode away. His companion, thinking the boy's hurt worse than his own, concluded that he would stand a better chance of getting clear alone, and riding off on pretence of seeking the path, failed to return. Jonathan was now wholly deserted. Wounded, ignorant even of the direction of his home, surrounded by bloodthirsty Indians, and weak with hunger, he pushed desperately on. He was near fainting once, when he heard some Indians running about and whooping near by; but they did not discover him, and a nutmeg which he had in his pocket revived him for a time.

After straying some distance farther he swooned in good earnest, and fell from his horse. When he came to he found that he had retained his hold on the reins, and that the animal stood quietly beside him. He tied him to a tree, and lay down again; but he soon grew so weak that he abandoned all hope of escape, and out of pity loosed the horse and let him go. He succeeded in kindling a fire by flashing powder in the pan of his gun. It spread in the dry leaves and burned his hands and face severely. Feeling sure that the Indians would be attracted by the smoke and come and kill him, he threw away his powder-horn and bullets, keeping only ammunition for a single shot. Then he stopped his wound with tow, bound it up with his neckcloth, and went to sleep.

In the morning he found that the bleeding had stopped and that he was much stronger. He managed to find a path which led him to a river which he remembered to have crossed on the way to the camp. With great pain and difficulty, leaning on his gun, the lock of which he was careful to keep dry, he waded through it, and fell exhausted on the farther bank. While he lay there an Indian in a canoe appeared, and the boy, who could neither fight nor run, gave himself up for lost. But he remembered the three Indians in the woods, and putting a bold face on the matter, aimed his gun, though its barrel was choked with sand. The savage, thinking he was about to shoot, leaped overboard, leaving his own gun in the canoe, and ran to tell his friends that the white men were coming again.

Jonathan knew that pursuit was certain, and as it was broad daylight, and he could only hobble at best, he assured himself that there was no hope for him. Nevertheless he looked about for a hiding-place, and presently, a little distance away, noticed two trees which, undermined by the current, had fallen forward into the stream close together. A mass of driftwood had lodged on their trunks. Jonathan got back into the water so as to leave no tracks, and creeping between the trunks under the driftwood, found a space large enough to permit him to breathe. In a few minutes the Indians arrived in search of him, as he had expected. They ransacked the whole neighborhood, even running out upon the mat of driftwood over his head, and causing the trees to sink with their weight so as to thrust his head under water; but they could find no trace of him, and at last retired, completely outwitted.

The boy limped on, tortured by hunger and thirst, and so giddy with weakness that he could proceed but a short distance without stopping to rest. Happily he saw no more of the Indians, and at last, on the third day of his painful journey, he arrived at Hadley, where he was welcomed as one risen from the dead.

The story of his escape was told for years around the wide fireplaces throughout the country-side, and was thought so remarkable that one who heard it, unwilling that the record of so much coolness and courage should be lost, wrote it down for future generations of boys to read.

V
THE CROWN OF AN AMERICAN QUEEN IN THE DAYS OF BACON'S REBELLION IN VIRGINIA

In the age when America was but a name and Virginia only a hamlet, there was a dusky queen who wore a silver crown by order of his most sacred Majesty King Charles II., King of England, Scotland, France, Ireland, and Virginia.

There are few distinct Indian personalities. Powhatan, Pocahontas, Opechancanough, Totopotomoi and his wife, the Queen of the Pamunkeys, are savage heroes who sentinel the seventeenth century; they all belonged to the Pamunkey tribe of the great Powhatan Confederacy, the most powerful Indian combination that ever existed.

When the boisterous and heroic Nathaniel Bacon[A] was in the flush of his wonderful success, and had brought his followers to Jamestown, he demanded of the Governor redress for Indian depredations and outrages. When the Assembly in council was sitting, the Queen of the Pamunkeys came in, leading her son by the hand. She came to tell of grievances also. She wore a dress of black and white wampum peake and a mantle of deerskin, "cut in a frenge" six inches from the outer edge. It fell loosely from her shoulders to her feet. On her head was a crown of "purple bead of shell, drilled." She was a beautiful woman, old chronicles tell us, and she walked in with a proud but aggrieved countenance.

She sat down in the midst of the Assembly, listening eagerly to the arguments for the suppression and, if need be, the extinction of her race. And she remembered Totopotomoi bleeding for these people who would not recognize her rights. She arose and made a speech in her own tongue, eloquent with gesticulation; the refrain of it was a mad wail: "Totopotomoi chepiak!" (i.e., Totopotomoi dead).

Colonel Hill, the younger, touched a fellow-member on the shoulder, and whispered: "What she says is true. Totopotomoi fought with my father, and fell with his warriors."

But the Assembly would not listen to the poor suffering Queen. They wanted to fight more battles, and the Queen of the Pamunkeys must furnish her quota.

"How many men will you furnish?" asked Nathaniel Bacon. "How many will you give to fight and subdue the treacherous tribes which threaten our peace?"

The Queen was silent. She remembered her husband and his slain braves. She had fears for her son, and she would not speak.

"How many?" asked Bacon.

The poor Queen had her head turned away and bowed.

"How many?" demanded the famous rebel again.

Then she slowly turned her lovely face, and softly whispered, "Six."

Her answer infuriated Bacon, who considered the number contemptible. "How many more?" he asked.

The Queen gave him a glance of indignant hate, and haughtily answered, "Twelve." Then she gathered her robes about her, and majestically left the room.

Once more we see the Queen of the Pamunkeys, and now in fear and adversity. Bacon in his campaign destroyed the Pamunkey settlement—the same tribe which had so nobly assisted the English.

The poor Queen, terrified, fled far into the forest, accompanied by "onely a little Indian boy." Her old nurse followed her, but was captured. Bacon ordered the old woman to guide him to a certain point, but she, full of revenge, led him in an opposite direction, whereupon the rebel ordered her to be knocked in the head.

The Queen wandered about almost crazy, and at last determined to return and throw herself upon Bacon's mercy; but as she was rushing towards her desolated wigwam she came upon the body of her murdered nurse, which so affrighted her that she ran back into the wilderness, where she remained "fourteen daies without food, and would have perished but that she gnawed on the legg of a terrapin which the little Indian boy brought her."

So only a few vivid sketches of this Queen are preserved to us in history but they have gained for her a place as a martyr. In recognition of her own and her husband's deeds, Charles II. bestowed upon her a silver crown, with the lion of England, the lilies of France, and the harp of Ireland engraved thereon.

Savages are not averse to the baubles of civilization, and the crown which their Queen wore was a blessed treasure to her tribe for a hundred years after the Queen was dead.

The Pamunkey tribe, or a pitiful remnant of them, still dwell in Virginia, on the river which bears their name. They have a chief, and their own government. Annually they send tribute of fish and game and Indian handiwork to the Governor of Virginia. They are weakening physically, and pray for new blood from the Western reservation.

Once the tribe started for the West, carrying their best treasure, the silver crown. They came to the plantation of Mr. Morson, at Falmouth, and there bad weather and sickness made them halt. Mr. Morson attended to their physical wants, and allowed them to pitch their tents upon his land until their distress abated.

"What do we owe you?" asked the chief, when they had decided to return to their former Virginia reservation.

"Nothing," said Mr. Morson. Perhaps he remembered Totopotomoi and his sorrowing Queen.

"Then we will give you what we value most," and the chief presented to Mr. Morson the crown of the Queen of the Pamunkeys. For three generations it remained in the Morson family, and then it was purchased by the Association for the Preservation of Virginia Antiquities.

The crown is really a frontlet, and the Queen of the Pamunkeys wore it upon her brow, surmounted by a red velvet cap, long since destroyed by moths, and bound to her head by two silver chains.

FOOTNOTES:

[A] Nathaniel Bacon, patriot, born in England, 1642; settled in Gloucester County, Virginia, 1670; led an independent force against hostile Indians in 1675-76 in spite of Governor Berkeley's opposition; as the head of the republican movement he came into open conflict with Berkeley and the royalists; he captured and burned Jamestown in September, 1676; died the following October; known as a rebel, but the principles for which he fought were in the main those of independence and patriotism.

VI
HOW A BLACKSMITH'S BOY BECAME A KNIGHT
THE TREASURE-HUNT OF WILLIAM PHIPPS IN THE LATE SEVENTEENTH CENTURY

Sir William Phipps, Baronet; Captain in the Royal Navy; Captain-General and Commander-in-Chief of Massachusetts Bay; Governor of Massachusetts.

What do you think of all these titles for one man to wear? Surely, you say, he must naturally have been a great man to deserve so much distinction; and again you say that the conditions of his life must account for such honors; that he must have been of gentle birth, reared in luxury, his education carefully attended by excellent masters, and great influence brought to bear upon his King to advance him so far on the high-road of fame. Well, let us see if facts will sustain this thought.

William Phipps was born February 2, 1650, in a wretched log house on the banks of the Kennebec River. His father, an honest but ignorant blacksmith, was more dependent upon his rifle and fishing-line to supply his family with food than upon the occasional shilling that found its way into the smoke-begrimed interior of his rude workshop.

Without education himself, the father was unable to instruct his children beyond the simplest rules of arithmetic and the plainest spelling and reading, but these he drilled them in as perseveringly as he did in the terrifying religious catechism of that day. In the course of years, when William developed into a robust, courageous lad, he shared with his parents the duties of providing for his sisters and brothers by either shouldering the heavy fire-arm and plunging into the dark Maine forests in quest of game, or in taking his father's place and beating out the iron sparks, while the sturdy smith dropped a temptingly baited hook into the swiftly flowing stream.

In the year 1676, in his twenty-seventh year, the hero of our story received his parents' blessing, and left home for the purpose of seeking his fortune. With a hopeful heart and an exceedingly light pocket, he made his way to Boston, and found employment in the blacksmith-shop of one Roger Spencer, whose pretty daughter Charity soon won the heart of her father's handsome, stalwart helper.

So far we fail to find very much in the way of gentle birth, luxury, education, and influence. But then, you may ask, how, under such circumstances, could he ever have risen so high? Let us follow his career.

His lack of worldly goods was made the excuse for refusing the offer of his heart and hand that he made to the fair Puritan, and in the hope of improving his fortunes he forsook the forge and shipped on board of a merchant vessel to follow the adventurous life of a sailor. When saying farewell, he gave his promise to return in a few years with money enough to build a fair brick house for his lady-love in one of the green lanes of Boston.

The ship in which Phipps sailed carried a cargo to the island of Jamaica, then cruised between that port and England for several voyages. Owing to his industry and ability as a seaman, Phipps was after a time advanced to the position of mate. A voyage or two following his promotion he fell in with an old seaman who claimed to be the only survivor of a Spanish vessel containing immense treasure that had been wrecked on one of the coral islands in the West Indies some years before. It appears that this treasure-ship had sailed from the coast of South America, freighted with a cargo of silver which had been dug out of the mines and cast into bricks to be conveyed to Spain. The sailor assured Mr. Phipps that the exact location of the wreck was known to him, and agreed, for a certain share of the profits, to conduct an expedition to the place where the vessel had gone down. Believing the story to be true, the mate bound the seaman to secrecy, and gave him a berth on board his vessel.

Upon arriving in London, application was made by him to the King for permission and aid to fit out a ship for the purpose of recovering a great treasure that had been lost by the sinking of a Spanish galleon in the West Indies, claiming that he had accidentally learned the location of the vessel, and that he would guarantee to secure the precious cargo. After considerable delay a ship called the Algier Rose was placed under his command, and with a crew of ninety men he set sail. Upon reaching the West Indies a mutiny broke out among the forecastle hands, and Captain Phipps found it necessary to put into Jamaica, discharge all hands, and ship a new company. He now started for the scene of the wreck, but a day or two following the carpenter informed him that he had overheard the sailors plot to capture the vessel as soon as the treasure was recovered, and use the craft thereafter as a pirate. The Captain immediately decided to return to England, where he arrived after a stormy passage. Under the patronage of the Duke of Albemarle the ship was refitted, and a trustworthy crew put on board.

The second voyage across the Atlantic was pleasant and speedy, but just after entering the Caribbean Sea a new danger threatened the adventurers, for early one morning they encountered a large Spanish frigate, which at once started in chase of them. Captain Phipps addressed his crew, telling them that if they permitted their ship to be captured they would be sent into the interior of the country as slaves, to drag out their lives in the silver-mines. He bade them fight bravely if they wished to enjoy home and freedom ever again. The superior speed of the Spaniard soon enabled that vessel to open fire on the Algier Rose, which so heartily returned the compliment that some of the foreigner's spars were shot away, making her fall astern of her saucy enemy, who now succeeded in escaping. Without further trouble the treasure-hunters reached the island on whose treacherous coral reefs the silver-ship had been wrecked. Here the Algier Rose was safely moored, and search commenced for the sunken wealth.

The small boats were used to explore the reefs, and served as platforms from which the best swimmers in the crew would dive into the channels between the walls of coral on the lee side of the island, endeavoring to locate the spot where the galleon had been carried before she struck. As the water in these places seldom exceeded twenty feet in depth, the bottom would have been plainly visible from the boat had it not been for the continuous rippling and foaming of the surface water. Several weeks were passed in a vain pursuit, and at last, worn out and discouraged, the men positively refused to continue the work. By agreeing to abandon the enterprise and set sail for England at the end of another week, unless some success was met with, the Captain prevailed upon several of his seamen to aid him for that length of time.

Day after day went by, and the seventh and last day specified in the agreement arrived. Two of the divers had broken down under the strain, and now when the final trial was to be made the Captain called for two men to go in their stead, but no one responded. He then appealed to their manhood, asked them if he had not shared all their labors, and asked them to give him but one day more. The dispirited sailors made no response to the appeal, but the cook volunteered to go if some one would take his place in the galley. This man was a negro about thirty years of age, and had been shipped in England to act as a cabin servant on the Algier Rose, but the ship's cook having died on the passage out, he had been sent into the caboose to take the former's place. Possessing a powerful physique and being an excellent swimmer, he stood by his Captain that day, the sole remaining hope, and seemed tireless in his efforts to find for the disheartened commander some evidence of the treasure, which the seamen swore existed only in the capsized brain of the man whom they could see out yonder under the broiling sun guiding the boat in and out of the channels, while the laughing, leaping waters tinkled against the bows and ran in gurgling, mocking glee along the side. The negro would dive into the sea, and a few moments later reappear; then, as he swam towards the boat, he would shake his head in answer to the anxious, questioning look in the Captain's eyes. The boat would move on again a short distance, and while the rowers held it stationary a dark form would part the water and sink down and down among the startled fishes, that flashed away in affright from the strange creature whose darting arms seemed to grasp at them as they shot for safety among the branches of coral underbush.

The morning has passed gloomily away, and the negro plunges over the side for the last time before the men row back to the ship for dinner. Suddenly a black face in which is set two wildly rolling eyes bobs up alongside the boat, and a voice choking for breath and broken with excitement manages to gasp, "Him down thar, Massa Cap'n; him down thar!"

The great treasure is discovered!

No more despondency now. No more aching limbs. Splash, splash, splash! The rowers have torn off their scanty clothing, and jumped over the side to prove with their own eyes the story brought up to them from the bottom of the sea. One by one men reappear, and their recovered breath is used to send such a glad shout across the reefs that their shipmates hear it over a mile away, tumble into the boats alongside, and pull madly out to them; then learning the joyful news, they break into cheers, kick off their garments, and overboard they also go to see the ingots of silver scattered over the white sand amid the torn and broken remnants of the wreck.

During the two weeks that followed the crew of the Algier Rose worked zealously at recovering the wealth that the Spaniards had taken such pains to garner from the mountain range just back of the coast. A shallow network bag was hitched together by the seamen for the purpose of holding the bars of silver that the divers would throw into it. Those manning the float that had been constructed would lower the rope cradle until it rested on the bottom; then the diver would thrust his feet into a pair of heavy lead slippers and drop through the hole in the centre of the raft which was anchored above the wreck. An instant later, when the bed of sand was reached, the diver would quickly select and throw a brick of metal into the basket, drop his clumsy foot-gear into the same receptacle, and then, relieved of the weight which had held him down, he would shoot up to the surface of the water. Accepting his reappearance as a signal, the men on the float would haul up the net, lift out the treasure, and pass it into the small boats to be carried to the ship. At the end of a fortnight, when the divers reported that the last bar had been gathered, the Captain calculated that he had recovered fully thirty tons of pure silver.

The stone in the lower hold was thrown overboard to make room for the noble ballast, which was carefully stowed and wedged in its mean and gloomy quarters under the decks. The Algier Rose now sailed for England, where she arrived safely five weeks from the day that her anchor had been hove up from its resting-place on the white coral bed off the treasure island.

Captain Phipps's share of the profits was very large, but the exact amount is unknown. In addition to a princely revenue, the King was so much pleased with him for bringing such wealth into the country that he conferred on him the honor of knighthood, and to reward him still further for having beaten off the Spanish man-of-war, his Majesty was pleased to grant him a commission as Captain in the Royal Navy.

Sir William soon sailed for Boston in command of a fine frigate, and a reunion with the now-envied Charity was speedily followed by the tying of a true-lover's knot before the altar of the old meeting-house near the fort. A few months later the former blacksmith's boy redeemed his promise by presenting to my lady "a fair brick house in one of the green lanes of Boston." This residence, which was erected on Salem Street, stood until a few years ago, being last used as an orphan asylum for boys. In 1690 Sir William was named by the King, Captain-General and Commander-in-Chief of Massachusetts Bay, and several years later received a royal patent as Governor of Massachusetts.

VII
THE GIRL CAPTAIN OF CASTLE DANGEROUS
HOW THREE CHILDREN FOUGHT THE IROQUOIS IN 1692

Among all the incidents of endurance and pluck set forth in the annals of the history of North America, few can be found more remarkable than that which is contained in some very dusty pages to be read in quaint French in a Paris library, or in the transcription of them by one of our own historical authors—the "Statement of Mademoiselle Magdeleine de Verchères, aged Fourteen Years," daughter of the commander of a lonely French fort, called after her father, which stood on the St. Lawrence River a score of miles below Montreal.

It was October 22, 1692. The strong fort enclosure, stockade and blockhouse, were open, and the residents were at work in their fields at some distance. M. de Verchères was at Quebec on military business. His wife (who was the heroine of another famous incident of those perilous days) had gone to Quebec. In the stockade were actually only two soldiers, a couple of lads who were the young girl's brothers, one very aged man, and a few women and children. Magdeleine—or, as we should now spell it, Madeleine—was standing at a considerable distance from the open gate of the fort with a servant, little suspecting any danger.

All at once a rattle of arms from the direction where some of the agriculturists were busy startled her. It was repeated. She began to see men running in terror in the far-away fields. At the same moment the serving-man beside her, equally astonished, exclaimed, "Run, Mademoiselle, run; the Iroquois are upon us!" The young girl looked where he pointed, and lo! a troop of some forty or fifty of the wily savages, thinking to surprise the stockade while their main band attacked those who were outside, were running towards the gates, scarcely a hundred yards from where she stood trembling. There was not an instant to lose. It was life or death for her and all. She fled for the fort. The rest of her story can largely be quoted from Mademoiselle Madeleine's own recitation, published at the time.

"The Iroquois who chased me, seeing that they could not catch me alive before I reached the gate, stopped and fired at me. The bullets whistled about my ears, and [as she says, dryly] made the time seem very long. As soon as I was near enough to be heard, I cried out, 'To arms! to arms!' hoping that somebody would come out and help me, but it was no use. The two soldiers in the fort were so terrified that they had hidden within the block-house.

"At the gate I found two women crying for their husbands, who had just been killed. I forced them to go in and shut the gate. I next thought what I could do to save myself and the few people with me. I went to inspect the fort, and found that several palisades had fallen down and left openings by which the enemy could easily get in. I ordered them to be set up again, and helped to carry them myself."

It may be asked how there was sufficient time for this necessary work. But it must be remembered that the Indians seldom came directly to the stockade in daylight, dreading concealed defenders greatly, and in the present instance they were ignorant of the singularly unprotected state of this fort. So the brave little girl was able to prepare for the worst with all her wonderful presence of mind and courage. She continues:

"When all the breaches were stopped, I went to the block-house, where the ammunition is kept, and here I found the two soldiers, one hiding in a corner, and the other with a lighted match in his hand. 'What are you going to do with that match?' I asked. He answered, 'Set off the powder and blow us all up!' 'You are a miserable coward,' said I. 'Go out of this place!' I spoke so resolutely that he obeyed. I then threw off my bonnet, and after putting on a hat and taking a gun I said to my brothers: 'Let us fight to the death. We are fighting for our country and our religion. Remember that our father has taught you that gentlemen are born to shed their blood for the service of God and the King.'"

Getting her little company together in the stockade, and discovering the Iroquois moving about the fields, and either pursuing the unfortunate men and women in them, or else discussing the best means of advancing, Madeleine began firing at them from various loop-holes, and directed a cannon to be discharged to deter them from coming nearer, and at the same time to spread the alarm over the vicinity. The women and children shrieked and clamored. She made them be silent, for fear of letting the redskins suspect the situation. The foe drew back and remained quiet for a time, and as they did this a canoe with several persons in it was seen out upon the river coming swiftly to the dock near the fort. It was evident that those in it did not suspect the danger that was so near, whatever else they had heard. It was possible to save them from slaughter, and at the same time add the settler she recognized in the canoe, with his family, to the little garrison. Madeleine went out alone—none other dared—from the stockade to the dock, and received them.

The Indians, seeing only a little girl meet the new arrivals, feared a grand sortie if they dashed out of their ambush, and allowed Madeleine to escort the new-comers—a settler named Fontaine and his party—into the fort gates unhurt. She had hoped for this, and was overjoyed at her success. Her garrison now numbered six. She goes on:

"Strengthened by this reinforcement, I ordered that the enemy should be fired on whenever they showed themselves. After sunset a violent northeast wind began to blow, accompanied by snow and hail, which told us we should have a terrible night. The Iroquois were all this time lurking about us, and I judged by their movements that, instead of being deterred by the storm, they would climb into the fort under cover of the darkness. I assembled all my troop (that is to say, six persons), and spoke to them thus: 'God has saved us to-day from the hands of our foes, but we must take care not to fall into their snares to-night. As for me, I want you to see that I am not afraid. I will take charge of the fort, with the old man [she adds that he was eighty, and had never fired a gun, but he could probably carry an alarm]; and you, Pierre Fontaine, with La Bonté and Gachet, go to the block-house with the women and children, because that is the strongest place; and if I am taken, don't surrender, even if I am cut to pieces and burned before your eyes. The enemy cannot hurt you in the block-house, if you make the least show of fight.'

"I placed my young brothers on two of the bastions, the old man on the third, and I took the fourth; and all night, in spite of wind, snow, and hail, the cries of 'All's well!' were kept up from the block-house to the fort, and from the fort to the block-house. One would have thought that the place was full of soldiers. The Iroquois believed so, and were completely deceived, as they confessed afterwards to M. de Callières, to whom they told that they had held a council to make a plan for capturing the fort in the night, but had done nothing because such a constant watch was kept.

"About one o'clock in the morning the sentinel [the old man] on the bastion by the gate called out, 'Mademoiselle, I hear something!' I went to him to find out what it was, and by the help of the snow which covered the ground I could see in the darkness a number of cattle, the miserable remnant that the Iroquois had left us. The others wanted to open the gate and let them in, but I answered: 'No. You don't know all the tricks of the savages. They are, no doubt, following the cattle, covered with skins of such animals, so as to get into the fort if we are foolish enough to open the gate for them.' Nevertheless, after taking every precaution, I decided that we might open it without risk.

"At last the daylight came again, and as the darkness disappeared our anxieties seemed to disappear with it. Everybody took courage excepting Madame Marguerite, wife of the Sieur Fontaine, who, being extremely timid, as all Parisian women are, asked her husband to carry her to another fort. [A silly request, certainly.] He said, 'I will never abandon this fort while Mademoiselle Madeleine is here.' I answered him that I would rather die than give it up to the enemy, and that it was of the greatest importance that they should never get possession of any French fort, because if they took one they would think they could get others, and would grow more bold and presumptuous than ever.

"I may say, with truth, that I did not eat nor sleep for twice twenty-four hours. I did not go once into my father's house, but kept always on the bastion, or went to the block-house to see how the people there were behaving. I always kept a cheerful and smiling face, and encouraged my little company with the hope of speedy succor.

"We were one week in constant alarm, with the enemy always about us. At last M. de la Monnerie, a lieutenant sent by M. de Callières, arrived in the night with forty men. [He came down the river.] As he did not know whether the fort was taken or not, he approached as silently as possible. One of our sentinels, hearing a slight sound, cried, 'Who goes there?' I was at the time dozing, with my head on a table and my gun lying across my arms. The sentinel told me that he heard a voice from the river. I went up at once to the bastion to see whether it was of Indians or Frenchmen. I demanded, 'Who goes there?' One of them replied, 'We are Frenchmen; it is De la Monnerie, come to bring you help.' I caused the gate to be opened, placed a sentinel there, and went down to the river to meet them. As soon as I saw M. de la Monnerie I saluted him and said, 'Monsieur, I resign my arms to you.' He answered, gallantly, 'Mademoiselle, they are in good hands.' 'Better than you suppose,' I returned. He inspected the fort and found everything in order and a sentinel on each bastion. 'It is time to relieve them, monsieur,' said I; 'we have not been off our bastions for a week.'"

M. de la Monnerie in astonished admiration took charge of the relieved fort. The heroine's work was over. The savages fled, and not long after they were captured near Lake Champlain, and some twenty persons they had made prisoners at Verchères were brought safely back. The father and mother of Madeleine came from Montreal and Quebec, and heard the story of her valor and coolness with rapturous praise. She grew up to be a woman, receiving for her life a pension from the King of France as a mark of honor, and she died at an advanced age.

VIII
HOW MARC WAS MADE CAPTAIN
A RESCUE FROM THE "LORDS OF THE WOODS" IN 1695

One evening in the winter of 1694-95 a dozen young men were lounging around the fire in the big room of the storehouse at St. Maxime, a small settlement on the St. Lawrence River. The door opened and two others entered, brushing the snow from their leggings and moccasins.

"What luck with your traps?" cried one of the loungers.

"An otter and eight beaver," answered Noël Duroc, as he tossed a pack of pelts into the corner. He was a tall, straight young Frenchman, whose gay and careless nature looked out frankly through a pair of laughing black eyes. "But come, Madame Bouvier," he cried to the store-keeper's wife, "give us something to eat; hot, and plenty of it—eh, Philippe! If you want news, there's more than news of traps—it's of the Iroquois. 'Tis said they're ready for a raid to the north—to make glad the hearts of their good friends the Algonquins and the French. So our old bear of a seigneur may do some hugging. But to-night he has other things to think of. Marc is home—came up along the river from Quebec to-day."

"Is he as much of a monk as 'twas said he would be?" asked Jean Bourdo. "You know the old seigneur swears he will have no monk's scholar around him—though he were twice his nephew."

"We have just seen Marc, and, trust me, he is the same jolly lad he was two years ago. You can make no grave-faced monk of him! But the old seigneur thinks him surely spoiled. 'Twere better Marc had not seen the monastery—not that I lack as a churchman; what would we do at St. Maxime were it not for our good Father Auguste, who taught us when we were boys, and keeps us straight now that we are men?—for if he had stayed here he would doubtless be our captain—a post worth having, now that the Iroquois are like to visit us."

"Who will be our captain?" asked Jean Bourdo.

"The seigneur has sent to Quebec for an officer—one that's lately from France, and that's been well trained in the King's army. The old man knows how much we sympathize with Marc, and so, being surly as a bear, he will have none of us."

"It may be a costly mistake, this putting of an Old-World soldier over us," said Jean. "'Tis true we have small knowledge of the science of war as taught in old France; but we can fight in the woods, and know how to beat the Iroquois at their own game, and I'll warrant that's more than this fine soldier can do! 'Tis a pity that Marc—a lad brought up in the woods, whom we all like and would gladly follow—should be kept back just because madame his mother sent him to school to the monks. But the old seigneur will have his way, even when 'tis to his harm!"

"So he will; and if Marc is to lead us, the seigneur must be made to think that it is his own doing. Come, Philippe," continued Noël, turning to the man who had come in with him, "you are older than the rest, and have a wiser head; think of some way of bending the seigneur to our purpose."

They talked till far into the night, and when they separated the young Frenchmen had the cheerful and impatient air of men (or boys, for so they would now be counted) who had planned an undertaking and were in a hurry to carry it out.

In the afternoon of the next day old Antoine de la Carre, seigneur of the score of log-houses and the vast tract of woodland belonging to the royal settlement of St. Maxime, marshalled his fighting force. In front of the storehouse was an open space, from which the snow was kept clear, and here the soldiers of St. Maxime were drawn up in line. There were about forty of them all told, half of their number being young men, voyageurs, and coureurs des bois; the others were older, heads of families who devoted themselves to the more peaceful occupations of fishing and farming.

"I have news," said Antoine de la Carre, "that the Iroquois are moving, so it behooves us to make ready for them. You older men shall act as a reserve; the younger ones I will organize into a company always to be under arms and ready to repel attack. Noël Duroc, I appoint you lieutenant, to have charge till the officer who is to be your captain comes from Quebec. Be active in your duty, and see that you leave nothing undone that is for the good of the settlement."

"We'll do what we think is best for the settlement, and he'll find us active enough—that's certain!" whispered Jean Bourdo, nudging his neighbor.

In the ranks of the younger men was a tall, dark-haired lad who had the same bold features that belonged to the old seigneur. All observed him, for it was Marc Larocque's first appearance after his two years' stay in Quebec. He met his uncle's sour looks with unflinching, smiling eyes, and the settlers whispered among themselves that the old seigneur would find it no easy matter to ignore his nephew—he had the De la Carre spirit, in spite of the monks and their book-learning.

That evening was a gloomy one in the house of Antoine de la Carre. The old man sat in silence, drinking deep draughts of red French wine; across the room was his sister, the widow Larocque, teaching their catechism to two little maids. He knew she thought him unfair to her son, who, by right of birth and his own qualities, had reason to expect a place of authority at St. Maxime, and this knowledge made the old seigneur more than usually irritable. When the children had finished reading their tasks and left the room he broke out:

"Ha, Madeleine, you look so solemn, doubtless, because of your dear Marc! Well, why did you send him to the monks to have a scholar made out of him? You know how I despise these long-faced readers of musty books, yet you must thwart me in this way. I'll not forgive you nor him. I had no fault to find in the old days—then he was a good lad enough, and a true De la Carre. But I tell you now, as I told you two years ago when you talked of sending him to Quebec, that I'll have no bookman for a nephew. So you've only yourself to blame if he be set aside. But you were always obstinate."

"Ah, almost as obstinate as you, Antoine. But I'll not trouble about Marc; if you'll not help him, there are others that will. In these stirring times a boy like him is not forgotten."

After a pause he burst out again: "What folly it was! Has a lad here, in our rugged New France, any need of court manners and monk's learning? If you had sent him to learn war it would have been different. But to a monastery! When a boy in old France, I was made to read Latin and dig into musty manuscripts till they nearly made a philosopher of me. But I had the good sense to turn soldier, and since then I've had no liking for monks and their learning. Madeleine, you knew all this, and remember now—"

He was interrupted by a crash. The door was burst open and half a dozen Indians sprang into the room. Before Antoine could draw his dagger they had leaped upon him, seized his arms, and smothered his shouts. Madame Larocque was quickly and securely bound hand and foot and gagged.

The Iroquois—for by their paint and dress the old man thought his captors to belong to the dreaded tribes of the Five Nations—worked noiselessly and swiftly; in less than five minutes from the bursting in of the door they led out Antoine de la Carre, his hands tied behind his back, and a piece of leather so fastened over his mouth that he could make no sound. The guards that should have been watching were nowhere to be seen, and the Indians, with their prisoner, quickly scaled the stockade, crept across a cleared space to the woods, hurried to the river, and were soon on the smooth, wind-swept ice and moving rapidly westward. "Where were those young rascals of my company when I needed them?—drinking in the storehouse or dancing in one of the cabins, most like!" growled old Antoine to himself.

He was as strong as an old bear, but his joints were stiffened with age, and he had difficulty in keeping up with the rapid pace of the Indians. "What sinews these Iroquois have!" he thought, as he struggled on. "No Algonquin could hold his own with them; they run as well as our own young coureurs des bois!"

When it became evident that he could go no farther, they stopped their journey along the ice and, turning into the forest, went about a quarter of a mile from the river's bank. Here they found a dense evergreen thicket and prepared to make their camp. A fire was built, and some strips of dried meat they carried were heated and eaten; then they stretched themselves on evergreen boughs which had been piled on the snow near the fire. A tall young Indian, who seemed to be the leader of the little band, now turned to Antoine de la Carre and, much to his surprise, spoke to him in French.

"Old man, eat and warm yourself. We have far to go, and you are not yet to die."

Antoine obeyed, and after he had managed to swallow some of the tough meat he felt better. "How do you, that are of the Iroquois, who trade with the English and Dutch, come to speak French?" he asked of the young Indian.

"A French girl was brought a captive to our tribe; my father, who was a great warrior, took her for his squaw, and she was my mother. She taught me the language of the French, and taught me also to listen to the words of the black-robed Jesuits who used to come south to teach the Iroquois. My mother loved my father, and bade me fight the enemies of his people, and so I am here. But I wish the Jesuit teachers would come among the Iroquois as they used to do. I liked to hear them talk in that strange tongue they called the Latin."

"Did you?" said Antoine, glad to make friends with the young Iroquois. "When young I was taught by the monks, and know some Latin."

"That is well," returned the Indian, with much satisfaction. "I too was a pupil of the monks, and always listened to them gladly. Stand up and repeat to us some of the Latin you learned. When the good Jesuit would talk in that tongue to my mother and to me, the words came like music, and then he would tell us the meaning—it told of adventures and battles and great warriors. Repeat to us this musical tongue."

Antoine de la Carre would rather have fought a bull moose single-handed; but here was no choice, and he stood up and did his best. That was not very well; for his voice was as hoarse as a swamp-raven's, and it was many years since he had looked in a book.

The Iroquois lying around on the evergreen boughs were greatly amused at his efforts, laughing at his hoarse voice and at his stammering over the Latin words.

"You do not do it as well as did the Jesuit," exclaimed the half-breed. "Be careful, Frenchman! Remember, I am no dull log of a Montagnais—I am an Iroquois, a lord of the woods, and will have no trifling!"

Antoine stammered on, getting more angry each moment; for to a proud old soldier like him nothing was worse than appearing ridiculous. But this was a matter of life and death, and he suppressed his feelings. "'Tis well my young scamps of coureurs des bois cannot see me now," he thought. "They'd never stop laughing!"

"Look more cheerful, Frenchman!" said the tall half-breed, getting to his feet. "What if you are to die to-morrow; surely death has no terrors for so great a scholar and philosopher! And come, when you are talking to warriors of the Iroquois take off your cap!" Antoine wore his black velvet house-cap, and as the Iroquois spoke he stepped forward and plucked it from the old man's head.

Antoine had been able to keep down his anger at their laughing, but this was too much for his small stock of patience, which already was sorely tried. He was desperate and reckless, for death was fairly certain under any circumstances, and it might as well come to-night as later.

"Insolent—take that!" he exclaimed, and he struck out savagely.

The tall half-breed, hit squarely between the eyes, went down as if before the blow of a sledge-hammer.

Several of the Indians sprang to their feet and seized the old man. The half-breed got up slowly, half stunned. Antoine waited for his tomahawk to strike the death-blow, but the half-breed did not raise his arm to strike. "Old man," he said, "if I were like these other braves you would even now be dead; but, as I told you, I am a convert, and the Jesuit teaches that one must not be too quick in anger—especially with the old and foolish. You shall live, at least till to-morrow; give thanks that I, like yourself, am a monk-taught man!"

Soon afterwards the Iroquois arranged themselves to sleep, one of their number being left as a sentinel and guard over their prisoner. Antoine's hands and ankles were bound, and by the half-breed's orders he was laid on the boughs near the fire. One by one the Indians, save the guard, fell asleep; but the old Frenchman was too nervous and excited. Finally his attention was arrested by an object that was slowly and noiselessly stealing out from the evergreen thicket. It crept straight towards the Indian sentinel, who lay gazing up at the stars that shone through the tree-tops. Of a sudden there was a quick, stealthy movement and the gleam of a knife: the sentinel's head sank back, and he lay stretched out, still and motionless.

"A skilful thrust!" thought Antoine. "I never saw a man die so easily."

The man with the knife crept towards him, and in a moment Antoine felt that the thongs about his ankles and wrists were cut. The man beckoned and stole away; Antoine followed, and then they silently made their way into the thicket—leaving the Indians sleeping in the white starlight, the sentinel looking most peaceful of all.

THE THONGS WERE CUT

"Do you know me, my uncle?" whispered Marc Larocque. "I tracked you through the snow. Follow me swiftly and quietly."

Back they hurried to the river, and then began the journey over the ice down to St. Maxime.

"I thought the Iroquois strong and fleet, Marc, but I see that none of them is a match for you! You are a brave fellow, in spite of the monks, and never shall I forget what you have done this night. But I wish you had thrust your knife into the heart of the leader of the Iroquois, an insolent fellow who pulled my cap from my head and laughed at me. However, I gave him a good buffet between the eyes!"

Soon the old man began to lag behind, and Marc had to grasp his arm to help him; so they ran on through the white winter's night. With ghostly wings the great snowy owl flapped across their path, and the wolf pack halted for a moment to watch them pass, and then turned away to hunt again for some stray deer or wounded moose.

It was almost dawn when they reached the stockade at St. Maxime. Old Antoine was exhausted, and had hardly strength enough to say to Marc: "Send a messenger to Quebec to tell the French officer he need not come. I have found a captain here."

Marc took him to the seigneury, and he fell into a heavy sleep, from which he did not wake till afternoon. The soldiers were then at their daily drill, and after he had eaten, the old man went out where they were. Tall Lieutenant Noël Duroc was drilling them. Antoine de la Carre gave them all a severe scolding for their carelessness the night before.

"If it were not for my brave nephew," he said, "I would surely have been murdered by the Iroquois. Marc, step out from the ranks. I make you captain!"

A shout went up from all the men, but old Antoine silenced it with a gesture. He was looking at Noël Duroc. "Lieutenant, your face is black and blue; how were you hurt? You were not so yesterday!"

"Last night, seigneur, an old bear gave me a buffet—and a good round blow it was!"

Antoine looked at him hard. "Lieutenant, you had best let old bears alone!" Then he turned quickly to his nephew. "Marc, has that messenger yet started for Quebec who was to stop the French officer?"

"He left soon after daybreak this morning."

"Ah! you were not slow in sending him." The old man paused, and Noël, who was watching him closely, thought he saw his mouth twitch under the gray beard. "But never mind; it may be for the best. You shall be captain, my nephew, and you, Noël Duroc, shall be lieutenant, though I think you both rascals. However, no bookman could run as Marc did this morning; and so I know he is not wholly spoiled by the monks."

"Bravo!" cried Noël Duroc, throwing up his cap. "Bravo! Here is a right good seigneur who knows what is best for his people; and a kind uncle; and—I'll pledge my word—a great scholar and philosopher too!"

IX
CAPTAIN KIDD
AN OVERRATED PIRATE

Of all the pirates whose dreaded top-sails appeared along the coast of America in the old days of the colonies none has left a more grewsome and romantic reputation behind him than Captain William Kidd, the New York ship-master, who was born in 1650. Legends abound of his boldness, his craftiness, and his savage and blood-thirsty disposition, and stories of the immense treasure that he accumulated, the dreadful murders that he committed in its acquisition, and when and with what ghastly accompaniments he buried it are still told over the firesides of 'longshore hamlets from Maine to the Carolinas.

Fiction has not neglected to turn this pirate's career to its own purpose, and one of Poe's most imaginative and thrilling tales is based upon the discovery on Sullivan's Island, in Charleston Harbor (South Carolina), of a parchment which, on being held to the fire, revealed a cryptogram of Kidd's that led to the discovery of buried wealth amounting to millions of dollars.

It seems almost a pity to tamper with the halo of romance and mystery which posterity has drawn about this worthy's brow, but the fact is that Kidd was an unready, unwise, and vacillating character, and that there was little truth in the romances told about him. Beside such dreadfully famous buccaneers as Blackbeard, Roberts, and Avery he appears a pygmy in his own "profession," and his career, when contrasted with theirs, seems colorless and contemptible.

As to the vast riches that he was supposed to have acquired, it is doubtful if in his whole course of piracy he was able to accumulate more than a hundred thousand dollars. One thing is assured—the only money that he buried on the coast of America amounted to not more than seventy-five thousand dollars, which he hid on Gardiner's Island, over against New London, and the last penny of this was recovered by Bellamont after Kidd's execution.

During King William's War Kidd, who was a handsome man of somewhat pleasing address, made the acquaintance of Lord Bellamont, the Governor of Barbadoes. The two were in New York at the time of the meeting, and as Kidd was a member of a good family and moved in the limited aristocratic circle of that day, the new acquaintances saw much of each other. Kidd's plausible tongue, fund of anecdote, and agreeable manner impressed the Governor so pleasantly that his liking for the shipman developed into esteem, and esteem into friendship. Through Bellamont's influence Kidd obtained command of a privateer, and a series of lucky events contributed to his reputation, so that when he returned to New York, after his cruise in the Gulf, Bellamont and his other fine friends hailed him with adulation as a conquering hero. He was wined and fêted, was toasted by prominent men and noble dames, and over many a steaming bowl and long-stemmed pipe loosed his glib speech in a way to impress his hearers with a fine notion of his indomitable character. Through the thick clouds of the Virginia tobacco smoke a great idea was born in Bellamont's hazy brain. Complaints were made daily of the pirates that infested the shores of the colonies. These pirates were rich with plunder. True, they were skilful and bold and crafty, but here was a man who by his own confession was more skilful and bolder and craftier than any of them. Then, should Kidd be fitted out with a fine ship and a good crew to chase these pirates and capture them, great glory would come to Bellamont's name, and great good to Bellamont's pocket.

The idea was acted upon, and the Governor and some other wealthy gentlemen purchased the Adventure galley, equipped her, and armed her with thirty carronades, while Kidd went down among the docks and the sailors' lodging-houses, picking out for his crew sturdy two-handed mariners, men long of the sea, blowzed by the weather, browned by the wind, used to the pike and cutlass—men like ducks on the shore and like monkeys in the rigging.

The ship was fitted out at Plymouth, and the great day of the sailing arrived at last. The Adventure pushed out into the stream, Kidd smirking and bowing and striking attitudes on the quarter-deck, the busy sailors swarming aloft to loose sail, the good ship heeling over farther and farther as canvas after canvas was spread to a quartering breeze, and an assemblage of fine ladies and gorgeous beaux waving scarfs and fluttering handkerchiefs from the end of the pier.

Armed with a commission from King William to apprehend the noted Captains "Thomas Tew, John Ireland, Thomas Wake, and William Maze, or Mace, and other subjects, natives or inhabitants of New York and elsewhere in our plantations in America, who have associated with others, wicked and ill-disposed persons, and do, against the laws of nations, commit many and great piracies, robberies, and depredations on the seas, upon the parts of America and in other parts, to the great danger of our loving subjects, our allies, and all others navigating the seas upon their lawful occasions," he steered from New York on his way to the Guinea coast, where his hunt was to begin. By the terms of his commission he was to take the aforenamed pirates by force if necessary, with all the pirates, freebooters, and rovers associated with them, wherever they were found. He was to bring them into port, with all such merchandise, money, goods, and wares as should be discovered on board. But he was strictly charged and commanded, "As you will answer the contrary at your peril, that you do not in any manner offend or molest our friends or allies, their ships or subjects, by whom or pretence of these presents or the authority thereby granted."

Kidd had another commission, called Letters of Marque and Reprisal, to empower him to act against the French, with whom the English and their colonies were then at war, and under cover of these he captured a French merchantman off Fire Island on his way westward.

Upon arriving at New York he began to request more assistance from his owners, complained of the size of his ship and his few guns, and, as he "proposed to deal with a desperate enemy," asked permission to increase his complement. This was granted, after some hesitation, and he finally sailed from New York with a ship's company of one hundred and fifty-five men.

He made first for Madeira, thence to one of the Cape Verde Islands, and thence to St. Jago, in order to lay in salt provisions and other necessaries. He then rounded the Cape and bent his course towards Madagascar, whose waters were the known rendezvous of swarms of pirates. On the way he fell in with three English men-of-war, to whose commodore he imparted his errand with much pomp and circumstance. He dined aboard the flag-ship, and left behind him the same reputation for dare-devil recklessness and determination that his valiant speech had obtained for him elsewhere.

He parted with these ships after a few days, and arrived at Madagascar in February, 1697, after a voyage of nine months.

At this time most of the pirate ships were out in search of prey, so, having spent some time in watering his ship and taking aboard provisions, Kidd tried the coast of Malabar, where he was equally unsuccessful in finding his quarry. He touched at Mohila and at Johanna, both famous resorts for pirates, but he did not succeed even in getting news of those whom he sought. The reason seemed obvious—the pirate of those days was a dangerous man to tackle. He had guns, and he knew how to use them; he fought with a halter round his neck, and was game to the last gasp. He was in the habit of beating the King's ships sent to take him, and he had a bending plank through the lee gangway for their captured officers. A fat, rich merchantman was an easier victim. Why not sound the crew to see if they would agree to a change of policy?

Some such thoughts must have been passing through Kidd's mind at this time, for with the gift of a brass farthing he could have purchased from the most guileless and affectionate native of Mohila or Johanna his entire confidence as to the whereabouts of his friends the sea-rovers, and yet after a cruise of many months in this infested neighborhood Kidd had no tidings of a single pirate craft.

But however disposed towards acts of violence, he had not yet the courage to put his wishes into execution. On his second voyage past the island of Mohila he passed several Indian ships, richly laden and too weak to offer him resistance, but he contented himself with casting envious eyes upon them and suffered them to go.

The first outrage that he committed was at Mabbee, in the Red Sea, where, after careening his ship, he took some corn from the natives by force. After this he sailed to Babs Key, near the Strait of Bab-el-Mandeb, where he first began to open himself to the ship's company, and to disclose to them his change of policy. But instead of coming out like a man and saying that he intended to turn to piracy, he hinted and insinuated and beat about the bush. "Unlucky have we been hitherto; but courage, my lads, we'll make our fortunes out of the Mocha fleet." This was the closest his pygmy heart could come to broaching the subject that occupied his mind. But his mariners met him more than half-way, and he found himself committed to buccaneering before he knew it. By the advice of his quartermaster (the first mate or executive officer of those days) he sent a boat to go upon the coast and make discoveries, while he himself kept men in the tops of the Adventure to look out for the Mocha fleet.

The boat returned in a few days, bringing word that fifteen or a score of ships were about ready to sail, and that they were well laden and rich.

Four days after this the fleet appeared; the eager lookouts reported them, and the men rushed to the sheets and halyards, guns and ammunition-lockers.

Now was Kidd's opportunity to dash in, seize a valuable prize, and get off with her; but he hung off and on, perplexed between timidity and cupidity, until by the time he had made up his mind to put his fortune to the touch his prey became alarmed and began to scatter. He then bore down on the nearest; but by this time he had been sighted by the two men-of-war of the convoy, and the sight of their black hulls speeding towards him, straight and steady and business-like through the flying merchantmen, was enough for Kidd. He fired a feeble shot or two, squared his yards, and made off before the wind for dear life, while the crew silently handled their tackle, and indulged in I know not what contemptuous thoughts of their commander.

But by the act of firing upon a friendly flag Kidd had determined his status; there was nothing for him now but to go on with his pirating. Soon he had an opportunity to show that desperate courage of which, by his own account, he was possessed. Off the coast of Malabar he met a small Moorish coasting-vessel. Having discovered that she was short-handed and unarmed, he became terrible indeed. He seized her and forced her Captain and quartermaster to take on with him as pilot and interpreter, the Captain being an Englishman, and the other, Don Antonio, a Portuguese. The men he used cruelly, hoisting them up by the arms, drubbing them with a bare cutlass, and putting them to other tortures to force them to disclose the whereabouts of their treasure; but all he got from them was a parcel of coffee and a bale of pepper.

He then touched at Malabar, but finding himself an object of suspicion he quickly went away.

The coast was alarmed by this time, however, and a Portuguese man-of-war was sent out after him. Kidd fought her for a while in a half-hearted way, but, though she was his inferior in men and metal, he soon had enough of honest combat, and got off by his superior speed.

He next ran down to Porca, where he took on board a number of hogs and other livestock for provisions, and paid for them in good British silver. He also watered his ship and otherwise provided for his ship's company.

He then stood to sea again, and came up with a Moorish craft, the master of which, a Dutchman named Schipper Mitchell, hoisted French colors, as Kidd chased under that flag. The pirates hailed in French, and were answered in the same tongue by a Frenchman who was one of Mitchell's passengers. Kidd then ordered the Dutchman to send a boat on board, and when it arrived at his gangway he asked the Frenchman if he had a pass for himself. The passenger replied that he had, whereupon Kidd told him to pass for the Captain, "For, by Heaven, you are the Captain, and if you say you're not I'll hang you!"

The Frenchman of course dared not refuse to do as he was ordered.

The object of the manœuvre is apparent. Kidd had not the pluck to go on openly with his high-sea robbery, but fancied that if he seized the ship as a prize, pretending that she belonged to French subjects, he would get into no trouble on account of her. He did not seem to take into account the fact that his previous conduct had already stamped him as a criminal, but appeared to think that as long as he did not openly hoist the black flag he might do as he liked with impunity. Indeed, his whole career as a sea-robber consisted of similar acts of fatuous and ostrich-like stupidity.

He landed on one of the Malabar islands for wood and water, and as his cooper was murdered by the natives he plundered and burned their village. He took one of the islanders and had him tied to a tree and shot, after which he again put to sea in quest of prizes. After being at sea less than a week he fell in with and captured the greatest prize that ever fell into his hands, the Moorish bark Quedah Merchant, of four hundred tons. From this vessel he got a cargo which he sold for more than ten thousand pounds.

HE PLUNDERED AND BURNED

The Indians came on board of him and trafficked, and he performed his bargains punctually for a time, until he was ready to sail; and then he took their goods and set them on shore with no payment, which was quite in accord with his despicable character. The Indians had been accustomed to deal with pirates, and had found them, as a rule, men of honor in the way of trade, so it was easy for Kidd to impose upon them.

The pirate put some men aboard of the Quedah Merchant, and in her company sailed for Madagascar. He had no sooner arrived there than off came a canoe in which were several old acquaintances of his who had long been "upon the account," as they called buccaneering. They belonged to a ship called the Resolution, which was commanded by one Culliford, a notorious sea-robber. When they met Kidd they told him that they were informed he had come to hang them, which they would take very unkind in such an old friend. Kidd dissipated their fears by telling them that he was in every respect their brother, and as bad as they, and in token of amity drank their health in a bowl of grog.

Kidd then went aboard, Culliford promising his friendship and assistance; and Culliford in turn boarded Kidd, and the two worthies made a merry night of it in the cabin of the Adventure, spinning their yarns of the deep seas and laughing at their enemies; and as Culliford was in need of some necessaries, Kidd fitted him out from his spare tackle.

The Adventure was now so leaky that Kidd transferred her guns and stores to the Quedah Merchant and got to sea again, but not before more than half of his disgusted crew had left him.

He touched at Amboyan, and there learned that the news of his conduct had reached England and that he was outlawed. Indeed, the reports of his misdeeds were so exaggerated that the English merchants became greatly alarmed, and had Kidd, with one Captain Avery, excepted in a general pardon of freebooters which had just been promulgated. Kidd knew nothing of this, but relying on some French passes which he had found on one or two of his prizes, and deeming his brazen assurance enough to carry him through any peril from the law, he made for New York. Here, by the orders of Lord Bellamont, he was promptly seized, with all of his effects, and was sent to England to be tried.

Here his conduct was such as to destroy the last shreds of respect that one might have had for his character. Instead of meeting his fate like a man, he begged and implored and whined and promised, but all to no avail.

He insisted much upon his own innocence and the villainy of his men. He went out upon a laudable employment, he said, and had no occasion to go pirating, but the men mutinied against him and did as they pleased. As to the friendship shown to that notorious villain Culliford, Kidd denied it, and said that he would have taken him, but his own men, being a parcel of rogues, refused to stand by him, and several of them even ran from his ship to join the wicked pirate.

But the evidence was too strong against him, and he was condemned.

When asked what he had to say why sentence should not be pronounced upon him, he replied that he had nothing to say except that he had been sworn against by wicked people; and when sentence was pronounced he said: "My lord, it is a very hard sentence. For my part, I am the most innocent person of them all, only I have been sworn against by perjured persons."

And so, in 1701, whining and protesting miserably, he was led away to the scaffold, and there paid the penalty of his crimes.

X
HOWARD THE BUCCANEER
A CAPTAIN OF MANY SHIPS

In the days when high-sterned galleons sailed the Spanish Main, keelless and lofty, and helpless in the wind's eye; when all the sailors wore their tarry queues and ear-rings; when "Down along the coast of the high Barbaree" there was no law but that of the Moorish buccaneer, a young man in the peaceful British hamlet of Barwich reached the age of twenty-one.

Thomas Howard was a youth of promise and capacity. He was handsome, burly, popular, and generous, and always ready for any adventure. His father, a gentleman of rank and estate, was dead, but his doting mother lavished upon him an affection as blind as it was deep, supplied him with an excess of pocket-money, and left no wish of his ungratified. The result is readily imagined. His old amiability deserted him, and he sank into a savage discontent that found expression in numerous acts of roguery and violence.

As he grew worse and worse, an old friend of his father's persuaded him to seek employment upon the seas, and purchased him a berth as midshipman on a trading-craft bound from Liverpool to the West Indies.

A few months of sea discipline shattered young Howard's patience, and upon his arrival at Jamaica he promptly deserted his ship.

He had still a few pounds left of his fortune, and with these he purchased admittance to the society of a gang of ruffians who frequented the beaches. One night, with some of these, he stole a canoe and went to the Grand Camanas to join a party of others of their ilk who lurked thereabouts with the design of going "on the account."

They soon fell in with those whom they sought, and, as the party now numbered twenty, they deemed themselves strong enough to set to their work, and accordingly began their preparations. At a council held the night when this decision was reached, the question of the election of officers came up; the men seemed about evenly divided in their choice of a captain between Howard and a tall islander named James. The latter was finally elected by a vote of ten to eight, while Howard was chosen quartermaster.

Their first need was a boat; in the offing at anchor lay a turtle-sloop with two small swivels mounted fore and aft. She was the very craft for their purpose, but how were they to get her?

Close inshore on the other side of an estuary a mile wide Howard remembered seeing a large canoe moored in the light of a patrol's campfire. He and two others swam over to her, cut her line with their sheathknives, and brought her away without discovery.

The robbers then boarded her, and, with two men forward and two aft handling the paddles, the rest concealed behind the high bulwarks, stole out silently towards the turtle-vessel. The nature of their craft was not perceived until they were alongside their victim, when, with a yell, they burst from their concealment and made their capture without losing a man. They then started out for booty, but for a long time their only prizes were turtlers, which supplied them with men without increasing their wealth. After about two weeks they met an Irish brigantine with provisions and servants for the Governor of Jamaica. They laid her aboard, captured her without resistance, forced her men, and made off with her, leaving her master the old turtle-sloop and five men to bring him to port. Not long after this they surprised a sloop of six guns, and finding her larger, faster, and sounder than the brigantine, they shifted to her with their belongings. This was the third time within two months that they had changed their vessel, but still the game of "Progressive Piracy" went on. Off the coast of Virginia they fell in with a large New England brigantine laden with provisions and bound for Barbadoes. They made a prize of her, and shifting their own guns aboard of her, found themselves in a fine vessel of ten guns well equipped for a long voyage.

While on the coast of Virginia in this ship they took several English vessels, from which they got men, arms, provisions, clothes, and other necessaries. As most of these ships had on board felons for the Virginia colonies, they took from them a number of volunteers besides their forced men, and they soon acquired so large a complement that they had no hesitation in ranging up to and boarding a Virginia galley of superior size and twenty-four guns. They got a number of convict volunteers from her, transferred their stores to her, and set out to sweep the seas in earnest. They steered for the Guinea coast, that Mecca of pirates, and made many captures, which not only enriched them but increased their complement. After they had been for some months on this ground they spied a large Portuguese ship from Brazil, whose thirty-six guns did not frighten them from the attack.

As they hoisted the black flag the Brazilian Captain became overpowered with fear, commanded the quartermaster to strike, and sought safety for himself in the hold. His mate, however, a New-Englander, refused to surrender, and kept off the pirates for the better part of the afternoon. His resistance was strong and well sustained, but the Portuguese finally fled from the deck, leaving him with only thirty men—English, French, and Dutch—and he was obliged to ask for quarter. The pirates then went down the coast in their newly acquired ship and made several prizes, some of which they burned and some of which they sank. As they now mustered nearly two hundred men, the only ones that they forced from captured crews were carpenters, calkers, and surgeons, whose services they needed greatly.

Off the Cape of Good Hope they took two Spanish brigantines, in whose company they proceeded, until they ran the Alexander ashore on a small island north of Madagascar, where she stuck fast.

The Captain being sick in bed, the men went ashore on the island and carried off provisions and water to lighten the ship, on board of which none but the Captain, the quartermaster (Howard), and all others were left.

This was too good a chance for the exercise of Howard's love of treachery. He brought the faster of the two brigantines alongside, tumbled all the treasure into her, scuttled the other, and made off with twenty men and two hundred thousand pounds, leaving the rest of his shipmates to shake their impotent fists and roar maledictions after his diminishing sail.

After rounding the Cape, Howard and his fellows went into a fine harbor on the east side of Madagascar hardly known to European vessels. Here they buried most of the treasure, and for a short time enjoyed the luxury of shore life. Wood and water were abundant, game plentiful, and the waters swarmed with edible fish.

It was pleasant to the pirate, after his long trick afloat, to lie on the yellow sands under the shade of palm and mango and tamarind trees and see the slow surf breaking gently on the beach. In his nostrils was the odor of orange and spice; golden sunbirds and crimson cockatoos nested above him, gaudy butterflies floated about him, and in the shallow waters of the still lagoons were long-legged curlew, busy kingfishers, and wild duck with tenderly shaded plumes. Behind him the tropical jungles blazed gloriously with trees of blooming scarlet and flaring yellow, about which twined gorgeous creepers of dark purple, and from whose leafy depths came the chattering of monkeys and the twittering of innumerable birds. Far off he could hear the smothered thunder of lofty falls, near at hand the plashing of rivulets, and seaward the deep voice of the Indian Ocean. The Malagasy women brought him cooling fruits from the mountains, the hunters came back laden with the flesh of wild cattle and pigs and great, feathery bunches of waterfowl, and the native king sent down to him rice and bananas, maize and manioc, from the rich store of his harvest.

After but a month of this happy shore life they set sail, and running down the coast of Africa met the English ship Prosperous, which they captured by a night attack. The Prosperous was a large, well-found ship of sixteen guns, and well suited to Howard's purpose, so he transferred his crew and stores to her and sailed to Maritan. They found there a number of shipwrecked pirates, who, with some of the Prosperous's crew, took on with them, and increased their complement to seventy men.

They next steered for St. Mary's, where they wooded, watered, and shipped more hands. Here they had an invitation from one Ort van Tyle, a sturdy Dutch trader of social ambition, to attend the christening of two of his children. He received them with hospitality and civility, but they had no sooner entered his house than they began to plunder it, and Van Tyle protesting, they took him prisoner, and designed to hang him, but one of the pirates aided him to escape and he took to the woods. Here he met some of his black; he armed them, and formed an ambush on a scrubby island where the river channel was narrow. The pirates came down in their canoe and Howard's pinnace, laughing and shouting, bringing with them the booty of the looted house and some captives, whom they set at the paddles. The canoe was overturned in the rapids just as they came abreast of the ambush, and the captives swam ashore and escaped, while the pirates clung to the sides of Howard's boat. As they drifted by, Van Tyle let drive at them, and in a shower of musket-balls, arrows, and assagais the helpless pirates were swept back to their ships, dismally howling with rage and mortification. In this affair two of Howard's men were killed, while he was shot through the arm, and two others were seriously wounded.

THE HELPLESS PIRATES WERE SWEPT BACK

He then sailed to Mathelage, where he designed to victual for a West-Indian cruise, but he found there a large Dutch merchantman of forty guns, whose captain curtly told Howard to get out or he'd fall foul of him. Howard's recent experience with Dutchmen had been unpleasant, so, as his vessel was not strong enough to cope with the Amsterdamer, he made sail for Mayotta, and passed down the bay amid a volley of gibes, jeers, and ingenious Dutch profanity. On his way to Mayotta he fell in with Captain Bowen, of the pirate ship Speedy Return, of thirty guns, and communicated to him the contumely to which a "Gentleman of the Seas" had been subjected. Bowen promised to avenge the insult to their honorable craft, and accordingly anchored in the dusk of the next evening within hail of the irascible burgher. The Speedy Return was a small ship for her armament and crew, and this, with her suspicious appearance, determined the Dutchman once more to exhibit the bold front that he could assume when there seemed to be no danger in it. Accordingly he went to the rail and bawled over the quiet waters, "Vot sheep is dot, and vy for you don'd git oud to onced?"

"This is his Majesty's cruiser Haystack," came the unruffled response, in Bowen's clear voice. "She has three decks and no bottom, and sails four miles to leeward and one ahead. Want to race?"

"Vot sheep is dot, and none of your tomfoolishness?" roared the Teuton, purple with rage.

"This is the Flying Dutchman, Captain Vanderdecken, and the crew's all ghosts," replied the pirate, in high glee. "Come aboard and cheer up our spirits."

This was too much. The Dutchman mounted the rail and shrieked, hoarsely, "I now asks you der last time for, vot sheep you is, vere you vrom, and vot you to do goin' about to be?"

"This is the ship Speedy Return," sang out Bowen, "from the seas, and I'm goin' to fire a salute."

The pirate then gave the word, and his ship roared out a broadside that shivered the Dutchman's rail, smashed his boats, and carried away his spanker-boom. The merchantman waited no longer, but slipped his cable and made off to sea, leaving the greater part of his cargo ashore, where it was promptly gathered in by the thrifty buccaneers.

Bowen now made sail for Mayotta, where he joined the Prosperous, and the two ships sailed together for the East Indies. After some successes there they returned by separate routes to Madagascar, for the purpose of revictualling and refitting, agreeing to meet again at St. John's and lie in wait for the Moorish fleet. They did this, and one of the Moors fell a prize to Bowen, but Howard did not come up with them till they were anchored at the bay of Surat, where they waited to lighten.

Howard came up among them slowly, under shortened sail, and as he concealed his men and kept his ports closed, they took him for an English East-Indiaman and suffered him to approach. Howard suddenly attacked the largest vessel, and after a desperate fight, in which he lost thirty men, carried her by boarding.

On this vessel was a nobleman belonging to the court of the Great Mogul. The prize itself was immensely valuable, and the nobleman's ransom amounted to twenty thousand pounds, so by this time Howard's fortune was well assured. He then ran down to Malabar, where he met Bowen and his prize, a fine, stout ship of sixty guns. The two captains with their quartermasters held a consultation (on the night of their meeting) in the cabin of the Speedy Return, and their future plans were decided upon over a rich banquet provided from the stores of the prizes.

The Prosperous they sank and the Speedy Return they burned, and in Bowen's prize they continued their depredations, the two crews being joined together. This made Howard's ninth change of vessels since he had taken to piracy.

As they cruised down the coast of Madagascar they came in sight of Howard's old haven, where he had buried his treasure. He became seized with a desire for shore life, and with those of his men who had lived there before with him, and with their share of the recent booty, he went back to his old stamping-ground to settle down. He was received with open arms by his old friends among the natives; he married a Malagasy woman, and for a long time lived quietly and peaceably, shooting, fishing, watching his herds, and cultivating his fields.

A missionary who was shipwrecked on the coast about a year after Howard's return worked on the pirate's soft heart so successfully that before being taken home on a trading-vessel that put in for water he had brought the gallant buccaneer into the close folds of the Roman Catholic Church and to a full realization of his unusually sinful state. After the missionary's departure Howard missed the theological discourse and dispute that had whiled away many a tropic twilight, and he knew not where to turn for an outlet of his intellectual activities. Finally the bright idea struck him that it would be both pleasing and beneficial to evangelize the natives. In a fit of religious enthusiasm he proceeded to this work with his usual prodigal hand. Unfortunately for himself, he used a club in the process, and this, coupled with his brutal treatment of his wife, made him unpopular among the Malagasy.

One night the docile aborigines fell upon him while he was asleep in his hammock, and left mementos of their presence in the shape of thirty-seven assagais stuck decoratively in various parts of his body. When found he was very dead, and thus terminated the earthly career of a treacherous and unworthy ruffian, whose only claims to our consideration were his good seamanship and Anglo-Saxon pluck.

XI
TEW, OF RHODE ISLAND
A FIGHTER FROM THE SEAS

On a lovely morning in the early part of the eighteenth century two vessels might have been seen approaching each other at that point where the northern waters of the Mozambique Channel mingle with those of the Indian Ocean. The day was mild and the wind light and variable. The ships rolled lazily on the languid swell, and a couple of leagues to the south and east of them the low, green shores of Madagascar were dimly visible.

As the vessels drew near to each other the smaller of the two, a large brig-sloop with raking masts and a narrow, speedy-looking hull, put down her helm, rounded into the wind, and ran the black flag up to her main peak. The other, a trim and sturdy ship-rigged craft, with something of a man-of-war look about her lofty spars and graceful lines, seemed little perturbed by this significant display of the pirate emblem. She hove to, however, and the two vessels lay rolling idly on the blue water a long musket-shot apart.

Before the sloop had time for any further demonstration one of the ship's quarter-boats was lowered and brought to the starboard gangway, and into her stepped a spare, dark, wiry-looking man of medium height, evidently the Captain. The boat shoved off and made for the sloop, the Captain steering, and the crew pulling with the long, regular stroke of man-of-war's men.

So far the ship had displayed no colors, and the peculiar nonchalance with which her crew had behaved towards the pirates excited the latter's marked apprehension. Could she be a public ship in disguise? If so, then farewell to the buccaneer's hopes of brave booty in the Indian seas, for the wind had fallen and the vessels were drifting nearer together.

The dark man seized the life-lines as they were extended to him from the pirates' gangway, and climbed up the ladder with catlike agility.

"What ship is this?" he asked, curtly, ignoring the crew that pressed ominously about him, and addressing himself to a tall man of a quiet but commanding appearance who stepped forward to meet him.

"This is the sloop Hope, sir, and I am her commander, Thomas Tew, at your service."

"And I am Captain Misson of the ship Victoire, lately of his French Majesty's service, but now from the seas."

The expression "from the seas" at once allayed the fears of Tew's pirates, for the buccaneers of that day thus characterized themselves in their answering hails.

The crew went about their duty, and the two captains entered the cabin, where they began a friendly conversation, and informed each other of their respective histories.

It seemed that Mr. Richier, the Governor of Bermuda, had fitted out two sloops on the privateer account, one commanded by Captain George Drew, and the other by Thomas Tew. They were instructed to make their way to the river Gambia, in Africa, and to attempt the taking of the French factory of Goree on that coast. The vessels sailed together and kept company for some time, but, a violent storm coming up, Drew sprung his mast and they lost each other.

Tew, separated from his consort, thought of providing for his future with one bold stroke. Accordingly he summoned his crew to the mast, and addressed them upon the subject of his plans.

He told them that they were afloat in a fine craft bent upon a dangerous mission, with no prospect of advantage for themselves, but only for their employers. That he was little inclined to risk his health and his life except for some great personal gain, and finally he proposed bluntly that they should throw off their allegiance to Governor Richier, and go "on the account," as piracy was called in those days.

The crew listened eagerly, and at the conclusion of his speech sung out as one man:

"A gold chain or a wooden leg. We'll stand by you, Captain."

Tew then made sail for and doubled the Cape of Good Hope, and as he entered the Red Sea on his cruise northward came up with a ship bound from the Indies to Arabia. She was richly laden, and carried three hundred soldiers to aid the crew in defending her cargo; but, notwithstanding her superior force, the pirates carried her with a dash, and shared fifteen thousand dollars a man in plunder. They then stood down the coast towards Madagascar, and the Victoire was the first ship they had sighted since leaving their prize.

Misson listened with interest to Captain Tew's story, and then gave him a brief account of his own adventures. He said that, having gone to sea as a sub-officer on the ship Victoire of the French royal service, he had participated in an engagement with an English man-of-war; that all his superior officers had been killed in the action, and that he had assumed command and sunk the Briton; and that after this his crew had requested him to retain command and go "on the account" for himself. He confessed that he had willingly acted upon their suggestion, had made several prizes, and established a colony on a bay to the northward of Diego Suariez, on the island of Madagascar. He informed Tew further that he was much impressed with the courage with which the Hope had borne down to engage a vessel so much her superior in size and strength as the Victoire, and that, as he could not have too many resolute fellows as his allies, he would be glad to join forces with Tew's men.

Tew answered that before entering into an alliance with Misson he would prefer to examine the workings of the latter's colony. Misson agreed to this, and the Victoire and the Hope sailed in company for Libertaita, as Misson called his new republic.

Just at sunrise the two ships passed between the fortified headlands that guarded the entrance to the pirate stronghold, and Tew, standing on his quarter-deck and following the motions of the Victoire, was astonished at the strength of the harbor he entered, and the discipline that seemed to prevail there.

With the timbers and guns of captured ships Misson had constructed and armed two powerful forts which stood on the headlands at the entrance to the harbor. On a little island, where the channel branched, a brown earthwork pointed ten heavy cannon so as to rake the seaward approaches, and far back of it, on the edge of the bay, the walls and roofs of a fortified town reared themselves orderly amid the green of the tropical foliage. Everywhere was the appearance of industry and discipline. On a beach near the town a group of sailors was engaged careening a small brig to scrape the sea-growths from her sides, another party was filling water-casks at a well-constructed reservoir, and the rattling of echoes of carpenters' hammers came from a couple of storehouses in process of construction near the water's edge. From a citadel in the centre of the town and from flag-staffs erected on both forts and the water-battery the flag of Libertaita fluttered in the breeze, vigilant sentries walked the ramparts with military tread, and as the Victoire and the Hope let go their anchors in the gentle ground-swell of the harbor, a battery of eighteen-pounders roared out a welcome of nine guns.

Tew was charmed with the appearance of the place, and upon going ashore with Misson had his favorable impressions strengthened and confirmed. The captains were received with great respect by Caraccioli, Misson's lieutenant, who admired not a little the courage that Tew had displayed in capturing his prize and in giving chase to Misson.

The colony at this time was peopled by over one thousand men, many of them having been captured by Misson in his prizes. Of these three hundred had taken on with him, one hundred were natives of the island of Mohilla, with whose queen Misson had formed a matrimonial and political alliance, and the remainder were prisoners whom Misson intended to send to their homes, and whom he employed in the mean time as laborers around his fortifications.

The day after the arrival of the captains at Libertaita a formal council was held. Tew promptly expressed his willingness to join forces with Misson, and was made second in command.

The question of the disposition of Misson's numerous prisoners was brought up at once. It was decided to tell them that Misson had formed an alliance with a prince of the natives, and to propose to them that they should either assist the new colony or be sent up the country as prisoners. On this decision being imparted to them, seventy-three of the prisoners took on, and the remainder desired that they be given any other fate than that of being sent up into the wild and savage interior; so one hundred and seventeen of them were set to work upon a dock near the mouth of the harbor, and the other prisoners, lest they should revolt, were forbidden, under pain of death, to pass certain prescribed bounds. The Hope lay in the harbor as a guard-ship, and the Johanna men were armed and put on patrol duty; but while the pirates were providing for their protection they did not forget their support, and large quantities of Indian and European corn and other grain were sowed in the fertile fields of Libertaita.

Soon after this it was decided to send away the prisoners, as they were too much of a burden for the infant colony. They were accordingly summoned before the captains and told that they were to be set at liberty. Misson informed them that he knew the consequence of giving them freedom; that he expected to be attacked as soon as the place of his retreat was known, and had it in his hands to avoid further trouble by putting them all to death; but that Captain Tew had agreed with him to practise humanity, and that they were to have their property restored to them, and were to sail for a friendly coast the next morning in a ship that was well provisioned but unarmed. All he asked was that they should never serve against him. An oath to this effect was cheerfully taken, and away the prisoners sailed to the nearest European settlement.

When they had gone Misson returned to the work of improving his town, and gave the command of his ship, the Victoire, to Tew, who, with one hundred and sixty picked fellows, set out to sweep the seas. He sailed down the wind to the coast of Zanzibar, and off Quiloa made up to a large ship which backed her main-topsail and laid by for him. Tew engaged her for four hours, losing many men, but finding her a Portuguese public ship of fifty guns and three hundred men, much more than a match for the little

Victoire, he attempted to make off. The Victoire, however, was so foul from her long service that she could not show her customary clean pair of heels, and the stranger, proving fast and weatherly, drew up with her. The Portuguese Captain, a gallant officer of great height and herculean strength, lay alongside the Victoire and boarded her at the head of his men; but the pirates, not used to being attacked, and expecting no quarter, made so desperate a resistance that they not only drove back the enemy with loss, but were enabled to board in their turn. At first only a few followed the Portuguese as they leaped back into their own ship; but Tew, perceiving the desperate resolution of these, sang out, "Follow me, lads!" and sprang over his enemy's rail. The Portuguese opposed the pirates firmly for a time, but to Tew's cry, "She's our own! Board her! Board her!" his men replied in continually augmenting numbers, and drove the defenders back to the main-hatch. Here a bloody conflict ensued, for the Portuguese Captain fought in the front rank of his men, and with voice and example encouraged them to combat. Seeing this, Tew rushed forward to meet him, and the two captains crossed swords with equal bravery. The crews paused to observe the duel, and watched with fiercely excited eyes the flashing sabres and shifting poises of their champions. The Portuguese had a longer reach, and was much taller and stronger than the pirate, but the latter had the agility of a panther, and was noted as one of the best swordsmen of his day. Time and again the Portuguese made a dash against his adversary with point or blade, only to be met with an accurate parry or a quick return stroke that forced him backward nearer and nearer to the open hatch. Finally Tew parried a furious lunge and delivered his terrible return stroke on the neck of the Portuguese, who threw up his hands and fell backward down the hatch. This ended the fight, and the crew of the public ship called for quarter.

With his rich prize, which yielded him one hundred thousand pounds in Spanish gold, Tew put back to port, where, notwithstanding his severe loss, his courage and dash were loudly acclaimed by the colony. Caraccioli persuaded two hundred and ten of the Portuguese to join the Libertaitans, and among them, to Misson's great pleasure, was found a school-master, whose services he at once devoted to the instruction of his negroes.

Two sloops of eighty tons each had been built in a creek, and when they were finished they were armed with eight guns apiece out of a Dutch prize, and sent on a trial trip. They proved to be fast, weatherly vessels, and on their return from their first trip to sea Misson proposed to send them out on a voyage of survey to lay down a chart of the shoals and deep water around the coast of Madagascar. As Tew was an excellent navigator he was given command of the expedition and of one of the sloops, while the school-master, who proved to be a good seaman and skilful surveyor, commanded the other. The sloops were manned with a crew of fifty blacks and fifty whites each, and their four months' voyage enabled the negroes not only to learn how to handle the boarding-pike, but, as they were anxious to learn and be useful, to pick up a fair knowledge of French and seamanship. They returned with an excellent chart and three prizes. Misson now determined to make a foray in force, and, dividing five hundred men, white and black, between the Victoire and the Hope, he and Tew set out for the high seas; of course a strong force was left behind as a garrison.

Off the coast of Arabia Felix they fell in with a ship of one hundred and ten guns belonging to the Great Mogul. This ship carried a crew of seven hundred men and nine hundred passengers, and towered monstrously above the low sides of the pirate vessels; but Tew on the starboard quarter and Misson on the port bore up gallantly, and engaged her. To the opening broadsides of the pirates she thundered an awful response. Soon the wind died out, and thick clouds of smoke lay motionless on the water; under its cover Tew brought the little Hope alongside, and, with his cutlass between his teeth and his pistol in his hand, clambered up the lofty side. He had barely reached the rail when he was severely wounded and knocked overboard by a pike-thrust. However, he soon came to the surface, and managed, at the head of a few of his men, to enter one of his enemy's lower-deck ports. In the mean time Misson had boarded the Mussulman on the port quarter, and a hand-to-hand fight was going on over the rail. Misson was hard pressed by numbers when Tew appeared from the fore-hatch. One glance at this murderous-looking figure, with bloody and smoke-grimed garments, rushing at them sword in hand from behind, was enough for the Mussulmans, and with a wild shriek of "Allah!" they broke and fled down the hatches, leaving the pirates in possession.

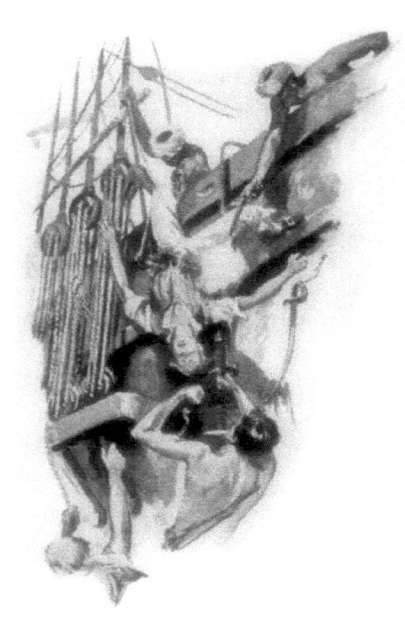

HE WAS KNOCKED OVERBOARD BY A PIKE-THRUST

This proved a most valuable capture, as over one million pounds, besides many rich silks, spices, valuable carpets, and diamonds were stored in the prize's hold and strong-boxes.

The prisoners were landed at a point between Ain and Aden, and the captured ship brought back to Libertaita, where, as she had proved a slow and unwieldy craft, she was taken to pieces. Her cordage and knee-timbers were preserved with all the bolts, eyes, chains, and other iron-work, and her guns were used in two strong water-batteries as an additional support to the forts on the headlands.

The colony was now in prime condition; a number of acres had been enclosed, and afforded pasturage for three hundred head of cattle—a purchase from the natives, who had begun to manifest a most friendly spirit—the grain was ripening finely, the storehouses and magazines were well under way, and the dock was finished.

As the Victoire was foul from long service and very loose from recent storms, she was docked and practically rebuilt. When she was floated again she was provisioned for a long cruise, and was about to set out for the Guinea coast when one of the sloops came in, schooner-rigged, with the news that she had been driven to port by five lofty ships, Portuguese, of fifty guns each and full of men.

The alarm was given, the forts and batteries manned, and the men put under arms. Tew was given command of the English and Portuguese, while Misson directed the French and one hundred disciplined negroes. Slowly and majestically the fleet swept on towards the pirate stronghold; as they came within easy gun-shot Tew leaped to the side of his water-battery, and with both arms outstretched stood waving in one hand the black flag, and in the other the banner of Libertaita, with its white albatross on a blue field. A storm of solid shot greeted the daring figure, but he leaped down unharmed, as battery after battery and fort after fort opened with a steady roar against the invader. The Portuguese dashed by the forts triumphantly, but wavered as they came under the fire at close range of the heavy guns of the water-batteries. They had thought to carry all before them with one bold dash, and after passing the headlands had deemed victory assured, but here they were in a hornets' nest. Under the dreadful fire from Tew's and Misson's skilful gunners two of the Portuguese vessels were speedily sunk. The others turned to flee; but they were not to get off so easily. No sooner were they clear of the forts than the pirates manned both ships and sloops, gave them chase, and engaged them in the open sea. The Portuguese defended themselves gallantly, and one of them, which was attacked by the two sloops, beat off the Libertaitans twice; two made a running fight and got off, and the third was left to shift as she could. This last, a fifty-gun ship of three hundred and twenty men, defended herself till the greater number of her crew were killed. Finally, finding that she was left to an unequal fight, she asked for quarter, and good quarter was given. Thus ended Admiral X's "holiday jaunt to wipe out a nest of pirates," as the Portuguese Commander-in-Chief had described his expedition in advance.

None of the prisoners were plundered, but, on the contrary, the pirate captains invited to their table the officers of the captured ship, and congratulated them upon their courage and ability.

For some months after this nothing occurred to interrupt the quiet of the colony. Finally, wearying of inactivity, Tew took the Victoire and three hundred men and sailed in search of prizes. Sixty miles from Libertaita he found a strange colony of buccaneers. The ship hove to and the Captain went ashore alone to make the acquaintance of the strangers. While he was absent from the ship a great gale rose and blew the Victoire ashore on a dangerous reef; she went down before his eyes, carrying with her every man of the crew.

This was not the end of misfortune, for a few nights afterwards the two Libertaitan sloops appeared, and from one of them Misson came ashore with disastrous news. The same night that the Victoire went down the natives had risen and destroyed Libertaita; Misson had saved a quantity of diamonds and bar gold, and fled in the sloops with the remnant of his band; they were now without a ship and without a haven.

The plunder and the men were equally divided between the sloops, and the two captains sailed in company for the coast of America. Misson's vessel went down with all hands in a gale off Cape Infantes, but Tew made a peaceful voyage to the British colonies. He settled in Rhode Island, dispersed his crew, and lived for a time unquestioned with his wealth. He might have reached an honored old age, with nothing to recall the memories of his past, but at the end of a few years he was persuaded to go once more "on the account." In the Red Sea he engaged a ship of the Great Mogul, vastly his superior in size and armament. During the action Tew received a mortal wound, but fought on as long as he could stand. When he fell his men became terrified, and suffered themselves to be taken without resistance. They were all hanged; and so ended the last of the Libertaitans.

XII
THE VROUW VAN TWINKLE'S KRULLERS
A STORY OF OLD NEW YORK

Clean, snug, and picturesque as a Holland town was our city of New York for some years after it had dropped its juvenile name of New Amsterdam and adopted its present name; but not so suddenly could it change its nature and Dutch ways. Dutch neatness and the Dutch tongue still reigned supreme. Substantial wooden houses turned gable ends of black and yellow Holland bricks to the front, until Pearl Street appeared like a triumphal procession of chess-boards; while no mansion in that then fashionable quarter could boast more big doors and small windows than that of the worthy burgher Van Twinkle, and the little weathercock on the roof was as giddy as any of its neighbors, and as undecided as to which way the wind actually did blow.

An air of festivity pervaded this residence on a certain winter's day in the early part of the eighteenth century; windows were thrown open, and Gretel, the eldest daughter of the family, followed by black Sophy, armed with brooms, mops, and pails, entered that sanctum sanctorum, the best parlor, to scrub and scour with unwonted energy; for to-morrow would be that greatest of Knickerbocker holidays, Nieuw Jaar, or New Year, when every good Hollander would consider it his duty to call upon his friends and neighbors, and the front door with its great brass knocker would swing from morning till night to admit the well-wishers of the season.

In the big kitchen also active preparations were going forward. A royal fire blazed in the wide chimney, and the Vrouw Van Twinkle, in short gown and petticoat, was cutting out and boiling those lightest and richest of krullers for which she was famous among the good housewives of the town: real Dutch krullers, brown as nuts, and crisp as pie-crust.

"Out of the way, youngsters!" cried the dame to a boy and girl lounging near to watch the boiling, "or spattered will you be with the hog's fat. Take thy sister, Jan, and off with her to the Flatten Barrack. She would enjoy a good sledding this fine day, and that I know."

"Rather would I go to the skating on the Salt River," said Jan.

"But that you must not. It I forbid, for very unsafe is it now, thy father did observe only this morning."

"Foolishness, though, was that, mother," argued Jan, "for last night Tunis Vanderbeck from Breucklyn came over on the ice, and told me that firm was it as any rock, and smooth as thy soft, pink cheek."

"Thou flatterer!" laughed his mother; "but not so canst thou pull the wool over my eyes; so away with you both to the sledding, and here are two stivers with which to buy New-Year cakes at Peter Clopper's bake-house." And diving in the patchwork pocket hung at her side, Madam Van Twinkle produced the coins, which sent the children off with smiling faces to the hill at the end of Garden Street, stopping on the way to invest in the sweet New-Year cakes, stamped with a crown and breeches.

Jan made short work of his; but Katrina had scarce begun to nibble her fluted oval when she spied an aged man, with a long gray beard, begging for charity.

"See, Jan," she cried, "the poor, miserable old beggar! How cold and hungry he looks!"

"Then to work should he go."

"But it may be no work he has to do. Ach! the sight of him makes my heart to ache, and help him will I all I can." So saying, the kind-hearted girl darted to the mendicant's side and slipped her cake into his hand.

"A thousand thanks, little lady!" exclaimed the man, fervently; "for I am near to starving, or I would not be here; and you are the first who has heeded me to-day."

He was evidently English; but Katrina cared not for that, and, carried away by her feelings, added a guilder, given her at Christmas, to her gift of the New-Year cake, thereby calling forth a shower of benedictions, although the old fellow seemed strangely nervous meanwhile, glancing in a frightened manner at each passer-by. As soon as the little maid's back was turned he slunk into a dark alley and out of sight.

"A silly noodle art thou, Katrina, thus to throw away thy presents," said Jan, as they hurried on. But his sister only shook her head, and smiled as though quite satisfied, while her heart beat a happy roundelay all the short December afternoon as she slid on her wooden sled and frolicked with the little Dutch Vans and Vanders on the Flatten-Barrack Hill.

Twilight was falling when the young Van Twinkles wended their way home, to find their bread and buttermilk ready for them by the kitchen fire, and their father and mother and Gretel gone to a supper of soft waffles and chocolate and a New-Year's-Eve dance at the Van Corlear Bouwerie.

"The best parlor, does it look fine and gay, Sophy?" asked Katrina, as she finished her evening meal.

"Dat it do," replied the old slave woman; "for waved am de sand on de floor like white clouds, and de brass chair-nails shine jest like little missy's eyes. 'Spect de ole mynheer and his vrouw come down and dance dis night for sure."

"What mynheer, Sophy?" asked Jan.

"De great mynheer in de portrait—your gran'fader, ob course. Hab you chillens neber heard how on New-Year Eve, when de clock strike twelve, down come all de pictur' folkses to shake hands and wish each oder 'Happy New-Year,' and den, if nuffin disturb 'em, mebbe dey dance in de firelight."

"Really, Sophy, do they?" asked the little girl.

"Yah, dey do. Master Jan may laugh if he please, but right am I. My ole moeder hab so tole me, and wif her own eyes hab she seen de ghostes dances."

"A rare sight it must be! I wish that I could see it," said Katrina; and later, when she went in to inspect the parlor, she gazed up with increased respect at her stolid-faced Holland ancestors.

"Much would I love to see them tread a minuet!" sighed Katrina again, and even after her head was laid on her pillow the idea haunted her dreams, until, as the tall clock in the hall struck eleven, she started up wide-awake, with the feeling that something eventful was about to happen.

"Almost spent is the old year!" she thought, "and soon down the picture folk will come to greet the new. Oh, I must, I must them see!" and although the household was by this time asleep, she crept out of bed, slipped on her clothes, and stole noiselessly down-stairs.

"Still are they yet," she whispered, glancing up at the pictured faces. "But near the hour draws, and hide I must, or they may not come down, for Sophy says that spectators they do not love. Ah, there is just the place!" and running to the linen chest she lifted the lid, and clambering lightly in, nestled down among the lavender-scented sheets and table-cloths.

"A very comfortable hiding-spot, truly!" exclaimed Katrina, as she placed a book beneath the cover to hold it slightly open; and so cosey did it prove that she grew a bit drowsy before the midnight bells chimed the knell of another twelvemonth. Then indeed, however, she was on the alert in an instant and peering eagerly out. Her corner was in shadow, but the ruddy glow from the hickory logs revealed the portraits still unmoved, and she was about to utter an exclamation of disappointment, when she was startled to see a door leading to the rear of the house suddenly swing open and the figure of a man carrying a lantern enter with slow and stealthy tread. An old man, apparently, with gray hair and beard, and a sack thrown across his shoulders. "'Tis the Old Year himself!" thought the fanciful girl; but the next moment she almost betrayed herself by a scream as she recognized the beggar to whom she had given her New-Year cake that very afternoon.

Slowly the midnight marauder approached, and then, all at once, a wonderful transformation took place. The bent form became straight, the gray beard and hair were torn off, and a younger and not unhandsome man stood before the little watcher's astonished gaze.

She was too dumfounded to do anything but tremble and stare, as the intruder seated himself at the table and ate and drank, almost snatching the viands in his eagerness. His appetite appeased, however, he seemed to hesitate; but then, with a muttered, "Well, what must be must, and here's for home and Emily!" he seized a silver bowl and dropped it into his bag, following it up with the porringers and plates, that were the very apple of the Dutch house-mother's eye.

Too frightened to speak, poor little Katrina watched these proceedings; but when the thief laid hands on a certain old and beautifully engraved flagon, she murmured: "The loving-cup! the dear loving-cup! Oh, my father's heart 'twill break to lose that!"

"Plenty of the needful here!" chuckled the burglar; but a moment later he had his surprise, for out of the shadows suddenly emerged a small, slight figure, and a stern voice cried, "Stop!"

With a startled exclamation the man fell back, and then, as Katrina exclaimed, "The loving-cup that is so old—ah, take not that!" he dropped into a chair, ejaculating, "By St. George, 'tis the little lady of the cake herself!"

"That is so," said Katrina.

The man reddened. "Believe me, miss," he said, "I did not know this was your home, or naught would have tempted me here; and this is the first time I have ever soiled my fingers with such work as this."

"Then why begin now?" asked Katrina.

"Because I was down on my luck, and there seemed no other way. Listen! For two years I have served as a soldier in the British army, and no more honest one ever entered the province. I did not mind hard work, but my health gave out, and at last the rude fare and the homesickness I could stand no longer, and three days ago I deserted from the English fort down yonder. The officers are on my track, but, so far, disguised as an old beggar,

I have escaped detection beneath their very noses. If caught I shall be flogged within an inch of my life, and, it may be, shot. Just over the water my wife and a blue-eyed lass like you are longing for my return, but, saving your guilder, I was penniless, and so, for the first time, determined to take what was not my own."

"Poor man!" sighed Katrina, the tears starting.

"To-morrow night the Golden Lion sails for England. Her crew, after the New-Year festivities, will be dazed at least, so I can readily conceal myself until the ship is out at sea. Then ho! for home and my little Jeanie!"

"And as a bad, wicked robber will you go to her?" asked the girl.

"No; indeed no!" cried the man, emptying his sack. "You have saved me from that, little lady, as well as from starvation to-day, for I would not steal from you or yours. Give me but these krullers to eat while I am a stowaway, and all the plate I will leave."

"Yes, that will I do," said Katrina, rejoiced, and she herself dropped the crisp cakes into the man's bag. "Now at once go, and godspeed."

"But first you must promise to mention this meeting to no one until after the Golden Lion weighs anchor at seven o'clock on New-Year's night."

"To my mother may I not?" asked Katrina.

"No, no, to nobody! Oh, remember my life is in your hands! Promise, I beg."

His tone was so imploring the girl was touched.

"I like it not, but I promise," she said.

"Thank you. Farewell." And again disguised, the deserter departed, as he came, by a back window.

Feeling as though in a dream, Katrina rearranged the disordered table, and then, creeping up to bed, fell so sound asleep that she never heard Jan when he awoke the household with his "Happy New-Years."

Gayly the sunbeams glittered on the black-and-yellow gables that 1st of January, and fully as resplendent were the maids and matrons of New York in their best muslins and brocades; while Katrina presented a very quaint, attractive little vision when she came down in her taffeta gown and embroidered stomacher, with her amber beads about her neck. Her face was hardly in accord with her attire, however, when she found every one demanding, "What has become of the krullers—the New-Year krullers?"

Madam Van Twinkle looked flushed and angry. "The beautiful cakes with which I so much trouble took!" she cried. "Ach! a bad, wicked theft it is, and a mystery unaccountable."

"Mebbe de great ole mynheer and his vrouw gobbled 'em up," put in Sophy.

"But what is worse," continued the dame, "in one big kruller, as a surprise, I did hide a ring of gold sent to Gretel by her godmother in Holland, and that too is whisked away."

At this Gretel also began to bewail the loss, and suggested that perhaps little black Josie, Sophy's son, was the miscreant.

"If so it be, to the whipping-post shall he go!" cried the enraged Dutchwoman, starting for the kitchen; but before she reached the door Katrina exclaimed, "No, mother, no; Josie is not the one."

"Why, mine Katrina, what canst thou know of this?" asked Mynheer Van Twinkle, in amazement.

"I know—I know who has taken the cakes," stammered the blushing girl; "but tell I cannot now."

"Not tell!" gasped her mother. "Why and wherefore?"

"Because my promise I have given. But when the night comes, then shall you know all."

"Foolishness is this, Katrina," cried the good housewife, who was fast losing her temper as well as her cakes, "and at once I command you to say who has my New-Year krullers."

"And my ring from Rotterdam," added Gretel.

"But that I cannot. A lie would it be. Oh, my vader, canst thou not me trust until the nightfall?"

"Surely, sweetheart. There, good vrouw, say no more, but leave the little one in peace. A promise thou wouldst not have her break."

"Some there be better broken than kept; but whom promised she?"

Katrina was silent, and now even her father looked grave. "Speak, mijn kind; whom didst thou promise?"

"I cannot tell."

"See you, Jacobus, 'tis stubborn she is, and wrong it looks. But list, Katrina; you shall speak this minute, or else to your chamber go, and there spend your New-Year's Day."

At this mynheer puffed grimly at his pipe, and Gretel would have remonstrated, but without a word Katrina turned and left the parlor. Ascending to her little attic-room, she removed her holiday finery, and sat sadly down to work on her Flemish lace, trying to console herself by repeating: "Right am I, and I know I am right. A promise once given must not broken be," while the New-Year callers came and went, and the sound of merry greetings floated up from below.

So it was scarce a happy New-Year, and the little weathercock must have pointed very much to the east if he considered the way the wind blew within-doors, for even Jan turned fractious, and declared, "There was no fun in calling on a parcel of old vrouws," and he should go to the turkey-shooting at Beekman's Swamp instead. But this his mother forbade. "Shoot you will not this day," she said, "for at fourteen, like a gentleman and a good Hollander should you behave. So start at once, and my greetings bear to the Van Pelts and Vander Voorts and Mistress Hogeboom," while his father carried him off with him to call on the dominie's wife.

This visit over, however, they parted company, and Jan lingered long in the market-place to see the darkies dance to the rude music of horns and tom-toms. Here he encountered two of his chums, Nicholas Van Ripper and Rem Hochstrasser, carrying guns on their shoulders.

"Thee, Jan? Good!" they cried. "Now come with us to the turkey-shooting. A prize thou art sure to win."

"But I started the New-Year visits to make!" said Jan.

"And paid them in the market-place!" laughed Nicholas. "Thou art a sly one, Jan! But great sport is there at the Swamp to-day; much better than the chatter of the girls and a headache to-morrow."

"So think I, Nick; but I have on my kirch clothes;" and Jan glanced down at his best galligaskins and his coat with its silver buttons.

"Not a bit will it hurt them; so come along." And thus urged, Jan joined his friends, and was soon at Beekman's Swamp, where a bevy of youths were squandering their stivers in the exciting sport of firing at live turkeys.

Nick and Rem did well, and each bore off a plump fowl, but luck seemed against Jan, who could not succeed in even ruffling a feather; while at last he had the misfortune to slip and get a rough tumble, besides soiling his breeches and tearing a rent in the skirt of his fine broadcloth coat.

"Ha! ha! What will Madam Van Twinkle say to that?" laughed his unsympathetic companions, when they saw Jan stamping round, his little queue of hair, tied with an eel-skin, fairly standing out with rage.

"Whatever she says, 'twill be your fault, ye dough-nuts!" he shouted, and would have indulged in some rather forcible Dutch epithets had not his cousin Tunis Vanderbeck come up at the moment, saying, "Mind it not, Jan, but with me come to Breucklyn to skate."

"Yah; better will that be than facing the mother in this plight," said Jan; and he was skating across the Salt River before he remembered that he had been positively forbidden to venture there.

"Sure art thou that the ice is strong, Tunis?" he asked.

"Not so strong as it was. The thaw has weakened it some, but 'twill hold to-night, if——" But at that instant an ominous cracking sounded beneath their feet, and Tunis had just time to glide to a firmer spot before a scream rang through the air, and he looked back to see the dark surging water in an opening in the ice, and Jan's head disappearing beneath.

While, in the twilight, Katrina sat by her window, thinking of blue-eyed English Jeanie, she was startled by a voice on the shed roof without calling, "Let me in, Katrina—let me in;" and on opening the casement a very wet and bedraggled boy tumbled at her feet, sputtering out, "Run for dry clothes and a hot drink, my Trina, for nearly drowned am I, and frozen as well."

The girl hastened to obey, and not until her brother was snug and warm in her feather-bed did she ask, "Whatever has happened to thee, Jan?"

"Why, on the river I was, and the ice it broke, and in I fell. But for an old cove who risked his life to save me, in Davy Jones's locker would I be this minute; for never a hand did Tunis Vanderbeck stir to help me, and unfriends will we be henceforth."

"And thy kirch suit is ruined. Does the mother know it?"

"No; for fear of her I came in by the roof, but I met the father outside, and angry enough he is because I went to the shooting and on the river. He says that on bread and water shall I live for a week, and to the Philadelphia Fair shall I not go;" and a sob rose in the boy's throat. "But what is queerest, Katrina, the old chap who pulled me out seemed to know me, and gave me this for you," and Jan produced a moist, soggy package, which, on being undone, revealed a single broken kruller, in the centre of which, however, gleamed a heavy gold ring.

"Good! good! Oh, glad am I!" cried Katrina; and hastening to put on her festival dress, when the clock chimed seven she went dancing down to the parlor, and creeping to her mother's side, whispered, "Now, my moeder, all will I tell thee."

In amazement the family listened to her story of the midnight visitor, and when she ended by slipping the ring on Gretel's finger, saying, "No common thief was he, for this he sent me by Jan, whom he has saved from a grave in the Salt River," the Dutchwoman caught her to her heart, sobbing, "Oh, my Katrina, forgive thy mother, for it was in my temper I spoke this morning, and a true, brave girl hast thou been. To think that but for thee our rare old silver would be on its way to England!" Gretel too hugged her rapturously, and the tears were in Mynheer Van Twinkle's eyes as he asked:

"How can I repay my daughter for saving the loving-cup of my ancestors, and for her lonely day above?"

"By forgiving Jan, father, and letting him come to the New-Year supper. Disobedient has he been, I know, but well punished is he, and he is full of sorrow."

"Well, then, for thee, it shall be so."

So Jan was summoned down, and a truly festal evening was held within the home circle, beneath the gaze of the old mynheer and his vrouw, who beamed benignantly from their heavy frames.

The Golden Lion sailed true to time, and never again was the deserter heard of on this side of the Atlantic; but for long after Katrina was pointed out as "the blue-eyed maid who saved the family plate and gave away Vrouw Van Twinkle's New-Year krullers."

XIII
THE SIGN OF THE SERPENT
A STORY OF LOUISIANA IN THE EARLY EIGHTEENTH CENTURY

The two Vidals—the father Captain and second in command at Fort Rosalie,[B] and the son Jean, who wore the stripes of a sub-lieutenant, though his face had scarcely a sign of beard on it yet—paced the parapet of the fort in absorbed talk. Below them rolled the brown flood of the Mississippi, gilded into tawny gold by the setting sun. In the splendor of that glow stood out in bold relief the galley which had arrived from New Orleans that day. Young Jean, who had been absent in the little Louisiana capital for two months, and had received during the visit his commission from Governor Perier, had been a passenger, and was now eagerly listening to the news of the fort.

"It is almost word for word as I tell thee," said the senior. "'Twas a month since that Monsieur le Commandant sent for Big Serpent to tell him the Governor's wish, but not, as Monsieur Perier would have chosen to make it, the beginning of negotiation. For all feel that it is not well the Natchez should remain in power so near the fort. But Chopart's words were like the lash of the slave-whip.

"'Does not my white brother know,' answered the Great Sun of the Natchez, 'that my people have lived in the village of White Apple for more years than there are hairs in the plaited scalp-lock which hangs from the top of my head to my waist?'

"'Foolish savage!' said Chopart. 'What ties of friendship can there be between our races? Enough for you to know that you must obey your master's orders, as I obey mine.'

"'We have other lands; take them, but leave the village of White Apple to the Natchez. There is our temple, there the bones of our forefathers have slept since we came to the banks of the Father of Waters,' pleaded Big Serpent.

"'Within the next moon comes the galley from the big village of the French. If White Apple is not then delivered to my soldiers, and your people gone, the great chief of the Natchez will be sent down the river, bound hand and foot, to rot in prison. Go. I have spoken,' and Monsieur le Commandant waved Big Serpent out of his presence."

"And do the Natchez submit? Will Big Serpent give up their beautiful village? Mon Dieu! It's a shame! It might have been managed differently hadst thou been made commandant instead of Chopart, mon père."

"Tut! tut!" said the father. "Chopart may carry his load, and welcome. 'Twould have irked me much to have done the Governor's will, for, after all, 'tis the sword, not the scabbard, which kills. Warning of treachery and conspiracy has come from White Apple, for thou knowest the old Princess had a French husband and loves his race. Yet her son, the chief, would bleed out every French drop in his veins if he could. I like not the signs, though only five days ago Big Serpent came to Fort Rosalie, and when Monsieur le Commandant flung the report of foul play in his teeth, the chief smiled like a baby in the face of its mother, and answered: 'Let my brother believe what he sees. On the seventh day hence my people will bring thee more than the tribute due for the time, thou hast granted, and will then give up White Apple to the French.' Yet Sergeant Beaujean, who has been at the village since, says there are no signs of preparation for departure, and that warriors are pouring in from all the outlying country. We shall know in two days more. In the mean time, Chopart reviles at all advice to keep the garrison under arms, with closed gates and loaded cannon. The insolent calls doubters cowards and old women. My sword should answer that taunt," continued the grizzled soldier, fiercely, "were it not for a bad example at this time. Big Serpent, though young in years, is as old in guile as the most ancient wiseacre of his tribe. So I fear to have thee go to visit Akbal now, mon fils, for the chief's brother is sure to be deep in any mischief brewing."

"Better reason, then," answered Jean, "to make the venture. Time flies swiftly, and I, surer than another, could go safely and might find a clew to hidden danger. Yet 'tis hard to break bread and play the spy."

Captain Vidal paced up and down, his features working in doubt, as the new thought forced its way to acceptance. He looked wistfully at his only son. "And thou wouldst go there and pit thy young wits against the Indian's devilish cunning? Well, it may do! Akbal was ever thy sworn brother and hunting comrade." So it was arranged without further words, but the father's convulsive hand-clasp, when Jean, in hunter's buckskins, bade him good-bye at sunrise next morning, proved how loath he was.

It was ten o'clock when Jean arrived in White Apple, which was about fifteen miles from Fort Rosalie. Eight miles lay through the black muck of a swamp where even the wariest foot and quickest eye found their way with trouble. The foul morass into which the river highlands sloped down on the landward side gave the shortest road. But its profusion of deadly reptile life wriggling and hissing at every turn encompassed the narrow path across the little knolls and tussocks which give the only foot-grip, with no slight peril to a blundering step. An easier route meant nearly double the distance.

Almost the first greeting was that of Akbal, but his manner was distant. He knew of Jean's long absence, but he asked no questions with the tongue, though his eye was keenly curious.

"I come to chase the buck with my friend once more before the Natchez seek a new hunting-ground," said Jean.

"Akbal not hunt to-day," was the answer, in broken French; "must listen to wisdom of great chiefs in council. They meet even now in the Temple of the Sun. Go; the woods are full of deer and turkeys; but first must eat, for Akbal's friend much hungry from his walk."

This hospitable dismissal discomfited Jean, for it seemed to close the gates to further knowledge. The breakfast of venison and sweet maize got no seasoning of cheer in the gloomy looks of the boyish chief. Through the door of the lodge the young Frenchman saw the lines of Natchez warriors stalking through the streets towards the temple, while not a sound arose in the village. All moved as silently as if they were a marching troop of phantoms. Akbal sat patiently as a bronze statue, waiting his guest's motion to depart.

In the centre of the village stood the temple—a huge, round structure built of logs, now wrinkled with years, and surmounted with a cylindrical roof thatched with swamp-canes, leaves, and Spanish-moss in an impervious mat. It rose twenty feet higher than the tallest lodges, and from one side extended an arched thick-set hedge, embowering a long passage to the adjacent forest, a quarter of a mile away. Here the priests and medicine-men of the Sun were wont to seclude themselves from the rest of the tribe.

The way to accomplish his quest suddenly flashed on Jean's mind. Once he parted from Akbal, seemingly to plunge into the forest, he could make his way to the exit of the long, bowery avenue, and thence come to the outside of the temple. There, it might be, he could learn all he wished, though with great peril to his life. So when the young chief pressed his hand in a sad and silent adieu, Jean, after a brief push into the tangled brake, fetched a détour, and found himself at the mouth of the passage. Through its dusky green light he moved cautiously forward to a coign of vantage. This he found in the shrinkage of two ill-fitting logs, which gave a space for seeing and hearing.

In the centre of the temple, on a rude stone altar, smoked the unquenched fire which had never died since the natal spark had flamed in a Mexican temple two hundred years before. This half a dozen hideously painted priests fed with fragrant barks and gums. Around them five hundred warriors squatted on the ground, and passed the council-pipe, while the priests mumbled and chanted, and a portion of the sacred band drew forth soft and monotonous music from long reed instruments. A rattlesnake, coiled around the right arm of the chief priest, swayed its crest with an undulating motion to the cadences of the music, and its bright eyes seemed to watch every motion with malign intentness, as if it were the guiding spirit of the council. The braves wore no war-paint, for their expedition was not meant to blazon its own purpose; but their faces, so far as they could be seen through the smoke, were distorted with such ferocity and lust of blood that they could dispense with the help of pigments. And so the priests chanted, and the players played their soft melody, and the high-priest stroked his serpent's hideous head as it curved and swayed to the rhythm of the tune, while the watching Jean was maddened by the delay and the passage of time and opportunity. At last, perhaps mindful of some signal from the high-priest, the snake darted its full length and struck with open mouth as if at some enemy,[C] Big Serpent arose from the seated ranks.

The Great Sun's oration to his warriors, spoken in the Indian tongue, was mostly jargon to the listener, but he construed enough of it to unravel the Natchez plot. Under the guise of paying their tribute, they would surprise the fort the next morning.

Jean waited for nothing more, but withdrew swiftly, and dashed into the forest. To reach Fort Rosalie as quickly as possible he took his way again through the noisome swamp which formed so much of the short-cut to the French post. He had found his way well towards the heart of that place of gloom and reptilian life. Inspection of every tuft of grass and weed now made progress slow, and Jean looked forward to a few moments of rest on the hummock twenty feet off which projected from the edge of a canebrake. How lucky, he thought, that he had escaped without detection! On top of this thought came the shock of a challenge, which made his heart leap.

"Halte, là!" and the figure of Akbal pushed through the reeds. His gun lay in the hollow of one arm, and from the other hand dangled a silver clasp with which Jean's hunting-shirt had been fastened, and which he had not missed till this moment. It had been found in the bowery lane near the temple.

"Better Akbal than another Natchez bring this back to his French brother," he went on, with a note of mockery in his voice. "Jan Akbal's prisoner; no hurt him; to-morrow set free."

Quick as a flash Jean's gun swung to his shoulder.

"Stand aside, Akbal, or I shoot you dead. It must be that or pledge of free passage."

The two stood like duellists with levelled weapons, waiting for the word, with stern faces and flashing eyes. This was not the time nor place to remember old comradeship and the rite of blood-brotherhood which had once been solemnized between them. That rite swore them to an undying amity, as if born of the same mother and they had tasted the red drops hot from each other's veins in testimony. But all this was forgotten. To Jean, Akbal was the barrier to prevent his saving the garrison. To Akbal, Jean was the agent bent on foiling his people's revolt from French oppression. But though their fingers touched triggers, they did not press them. Perhaps this hesitation would have lasted but a second.

But now Jean heard a whirring noise that disturbed even his tense train of thinking with a cold chill. He dashed his musket butt at something, but it flecked him like a giant whip-lash. A monstrous rattlesnake had fastened its fangs deep in his thigh. Another duellist had stepped to the fore. Akbal saw the snake spring, and was himself almost as swift in leaping the interval. He shook his head as he saw the enormous size of the serpent, which was in the deadliest season of its venom, wriggling with a broken back.

"Much bad bite, but try save Jean," said he, as he helped him across to the larger hummock. Luckily Jean's canteen was full of brandy, and this he gulped down eagerly, while the Indian cut away the buckskin from his leg. Two needle-point punctures, to be sure, seemed scarcely worth bothering about, but with an apology, "Knife much hurt, but good," he plunged the keen-edged blade into the flesh, cutting out the envenomed parts, and followed it by applying his lips and sucking at the wound for a full five minutes.

"Fine weed sometimes cure snake-bite. Big bush over there," and he danced across the bubbling marsh to a bog-oak with a thick mass of green at its base. The swollen leg and the pain which gnawed through the drowsiness of the working venom told Akbal that there was no time to be lost. Flint and steel quickly struck fire, and steeping leaves and roots he made hot tea and a poultice. So the Indian nurse fought the terrible poison in the veins of the patient all that afternoon and all the night long in the firefly-lit darkness of that evil swamp.

The panther screams, which mingled harshly with the subtler horror of things hissing and splashing in the fetid pools, passed into the dreams of Jean. Copper-colored fiends with serpent heads storming the palisades of Fort Rosalie and shrieking the Natchez war-whoop sank their long curved fangs in the body after the knife had rifled the head. "Mon père! mon père!

sauve mon père!" he cried, in his agonized nightmare, and then awoke, clutching Akbal's arm in a sweat of despair.

"Jan better now, stronger; no more bad dream," said Akbal, who recognized signs of coming strength; and indeed when daylight struggled into the swamp the color of the French boy's face had got back its lusty red.

"Come, come, we must hasten to the fort! I am myself once more," and Jean stumbled to his feet to fall back again with the sore stiffness of his wounded thigh. Then he remembered the meaning of Akbal's presence with a frown. The comrade-foe dragged the heart out of that look with a word:

"Go soon. Akbal no stop Jan now." He spoke with a proud sadness and submission in his tone. The serpent omen had come from the Sun God—not even that deadly bite could stop the young Frenchman's return, and he himself had been but the instrument of duty. So he carefully bound the sore leg, and they started across the boggy waste, Jean leaning on his arm and limping with a determined step. It took long to traverse that quaking and slippery road, and the sun climbed up the sky, and Jean became half crazed with anxiety, for his leg would only do so much work, with all the help of a human crutch.

At last they emerged from the morass and began to climb the upland, toiling on with the fiercest energy of Jean's tortured spirit. Hark! that was the sound of cannon from the fort, and then they heard the faint crackling of guns. "Too late!" half shrieked Jean Vidal, and he sank on the ground with the reaction, hopeless, helpless, and his face streaming with tears of rage and grief. Akbal dragged him to a sheltered place under a bank, and leaped like a deer up the hill. He believed in the sign of the Sun God, for the rattlesnake was the totem of the Natchez nation. He did not reason, in his simple, superstitious loyalty, that he could have left Jean to die of the serpent's bite. He only knew that he had been inspired to cure him. Now he believed that the further mission of salvation had been passed from Jean to him, and the French blood in his veins warmed to the dedication. The lives of the garrison might yet be kept from the tomahawk and the torture stake.

The fort was already in the hands of the Natchez when Akbal arrived on the bloody scene. The murdering crew gathered to his assembly whoop, with Big Serpent at their head. He told the story of the supposed miracle with fervent eloquence, and the lives of those who had not already fallen in battle were spared, including Captain Vidal, for these bloodthirsty warriors of the Natchez were pious in their way, and believed the sign of the serpent. Jean Vidal, too, remembered the stroke of that terrible fang with something like superstitious gratitude. Had it not been for that he and

Akbal would probably have slain each other where they stood, and every Frenchman in the fort would have been butchered or reserved for a more fiendish death. As it was, Chopart was the only one to suffer execution, and he justly expiated the deeds of a cold-blooded tyrant.

FOOTNOTES:

[B] Fort Rosalie, during the early years of the eighteenth century one of the advance-posts of the Louisiana colony, was built on the bluff where now stands the beautiful city of Natchez. This whole region for many miles up and down the river and inland was the seat of the Natchez nation, originally a Toltec race which had emigrated from Mexico shortly after the Spanish conquest.

[C] The rattlesnake was sacred to the Sun God of the Natchez, and was made to play an important part in their religious ceremonies, and the mummery which entered, too, into their war councils. Something similar exists in the rites of the Moqui Pueblos to-day—a race supposed also to have been of Toltec origin.

XIV
A DRUMMER OF WARBURTON'S
HOW A BOY HELD FORT GEORGE AT CAPE CANSO, IN 1757

A few hours ago I found an odd-shaped bit of blackened brass. The thing lies before me now as I write. It is a drum-hook. I know this for the simple reason that I was once a drummer-boy myself, and could not be mistaken regarding such a familiar object. I found this drum-hook among a lot of other odds and ends at the bottom of a well in an old, long-abandoned fortification. The poor scrap of silent metal brings to mind the tale of Rupert Haydon, drummer-boy in one of the old line regiments. His deed of heroism was performed at this same old fort which I have to-day been ransacking. Perhaps this drum-hook was once used by him! It is not at all unlikely.

By turning to your map of North America you can easily distinguish Cape Canso, at the eastern extremity of the mainland of Nova Scotia. Upon an island, about a mile from the shore and forming with it the harbor of Canso, is the grass-grown fortress which I have mentioned. The name of the island is George's; the fort has had several high-sounding titles. Why should it not? It is old—older perhaps than others with claims of easier proof. In 1518, over a century before the Pilgrims landed at Plymouth, legend says that Baron de Lery threw up the first embankments and claimed the country for the crown of France. Several times this fort has been besieged and captured, at heavy loss of life. New England sent expeditions against it. The bloodthirsty Indians repeatedly raided the place. In 1745 Pepperell and his valiant little army of Massachusetts, New Hampshire, and Connecticut militia remained here for some weeks, in order to acquire drill and discipline before moving upon the boasted Louisburg. And many another martial display has this neglected old fort witnessed, and personages celebrated in our history have walked within its ramparts upon occasion.

In the year 1757 Fort George, as it was then called, had as its garrison a small detachment from Colonel Warburton's regiment of foot. This trifling force was compelled to watch over a wide extent of territory in addition to the special place they occupied. France and England were again at war, and both regular expeditions and lawless guerillas abounded.

On a certain day in midsummer the garrison embarked upon a small vessel and sailed away to the relief of a threatened settlement. Rupert Haydon, the drummer-boy, was left in charge of the fort. With him were several women, wives of soldiers, and their small children.

"We shall be gone but a week at most, drummer," Captain Peabody had announced. "It suits me not to leave women and stores so ill protected, but the commands of my superiors must be obeyed. However, it is scarce likely that the enemy will have knowledge of the fort's weakness in time to profit thereby."

The drummer-boy stood at attention and saluted as the soldiers marched out through the covered way. With the aid of the women he hoisted the drawbridge and closed the massive timber gates. Then, scrambling up on top of the parapet, he watched the little sailing craft, her decks all bright with the scarlet-coated warriors, pass out through the narrow harbor entrance and disappear from view around the first headland. Scarcely had the transport so vanished, when Rupert's keen eyes discovered another vessel making for the harbor from the opposite side.

Mere supposition was useless. The newcomer might prove to be a friend. If an enemy, the chance of being let alone was problematical. It was now too late to recall the recently departed garrison. Upon the drummer's young shoulders lay the whole burden of maintaining the dignity of the English flag.

Rupert Haydon was only a poorly educated boy, but he must have had a great deal of latent talent. Even while gazing in consternation at the fast-approaching vessel, he mentally mapped out a plan of campaign. Hastily gathering the women about him, he explained the matter to them, and secured their aid. They were all well used to the happening of the unexpected, and inured to danger and fatigue. The wife of a British soldier has never had an easy lot. These rugged-looking though golden-hearted women donned some uniforms left behind by their husbands, and became, in outward appearance at least, full-fledged soldiers. The six small cannon mounted in the fort's bastions were loaded, small-arms served out, and ammunition placed conveniently to hand. One of the soldier-women mounted guard upon the ramparts, and marched up and down, in plain view, with musket upon shoulder. The English ensign was, of course, flying from the tall staff in the centre of the redoubt.

As the vessel drew nearer, the little garrison began to bustle with activity, and continued in the same fashion for some while. Two of the soldier-women would come out of the fort, stroll down to the shore, examine the stranger with an apparently mild curiosity, and then walk off together over the hills. Meanwhile the others, including Rupert, would come and go, disappearing and reappearing in all directions with the aid of the rocky ravines and clumps of trees upon the island. The idea of all this was to convince the new-comers, whoever they might be, that the fort's garrison remained unimpaired, and took no special notice of a single vessel. That the scheme had a certain effect was shown in the fact that the stranger came to anchor far down the harbor, well out of range of Fort George's cannon. It looked very much as if the appearance of these redcoats coming and going about the island had impressed her commander unfavorably.

After some delay the ship hoisted a French ensign, and a small boat put off from her side and headed for the fort landing. This boat contained three men—two rowing, and one in the stern holding aloft a piece of white cloth. It was evidently a flag of truce, coming to parley.

Although his worst fears were now realized, and they plainly had a formidable enemy to deal with, Rupert never wavered, but proceeded to dispose of his forces in the best manner possible. Leaving only the sentry upon the parapet, he marched out of the fort at the head of the others, as if they merely constituted a suitable escorting party. One of the squad he had equipped beforehand with a flag of truce similar to that carried by the man in the boat. The drummer drew up his little company in a single rank upon the glacis, about half-way between the intrenchments and the water's edge. At such a distance their disguises could not be discovered. Alone he advanced to the border of the pebble-strewn strand, and there awaited the coming of the emissary.

The latter was wary of approaching too hastily. He bade his oarsmen back the skiff stern first to within ten or fifteen yards of the shore. Then he stopped them, and, while they kept the boat in position with gentle strokes, he held converse with the intrepid drummer by means of lusty shoutings.

"I wish to speak with your Commandant," began the stranger, using good English, yet with a decided Gallic accent. "You are only a child.... A drummer-boy?... Am I not right?... I judged so by your small stature and pretty coat.... Inform the Commandant of your fort that I desire a few words with him."

"It is impossible," replied Rupert, coolly.

"What? Impossible?"

"Yes; I regret to say that the Commandant will not be able to see you at present. But I am his representative, and can also act as your messenger if you have something of importance to transmit."

"O-ho! We are very high and mighty, it seems!" retorted the stranger, angrily. "Like should have like for meals. I will not be so civil as I first intended. Tell your Commandant that my name is Rabentine—Captain

Rabentine. I have the honor of commanding La Belle Cerise, privateer, of St. Malo."

"A French privateer!" ejaculated Rupert.

"Just so," went on Captain Rabentine, looking from the drummer to his escort, up at the fort, and back again to the drummer, with some appearance of suspicion.

"I had thought you were a navy frigate," rejoined Rupert, promptly. "We are getting rusty for the want of a little fighting."

The other seemed slightly taken aback at this statement.

"Perhaps you may have such a chance even yet," he growled.

"Well, Captain Rabentine," cried the boy, courteously, "what else am I to say to the Commandant? For surely you took not all this trouble merely to let us know whom our visitor might be?"

"Inform him," shouted the privateer Captain, waxing wroth, "that I had intended simply to lay in harbor here and weather out the coming gale. That a good prize-ship is more to my liking than an empty fort! Perhaps there might even have been a case of rare wine sent ashore by way of compliment. But as he chooses to be so distant, and sends a drummer-boy as fitting ambassador to a French Captain, I shall give myself the pleasure of—But, pshaw! there is no money in this for my owners. Inform your Commandant that I have a mind to anchor farther up the harbor, where the shelter is good, for a few days. That I will not molest him if he leaves me alone. There you have it in a nutshell. Go, and haste quickly with the answer."

Gravely turning on his heel the drummer strode back up the hill, joined his waiting escort, and marched with them to the fort. He was gone upon this pretended mission some little time; quite long enough further to exasperate the privateer Captain.

"Truly 'tis a matter of wonderful ceremony," he sneered, when Rupert, after repeating the former precautionary measures with his escort, was once more at speaking distance. "All this folderol is wearisome. Your Commandant may regret not having sent an officer before we are through with the thing. Did you sufficiently impress him with the fact that I am not one to be trifled with? Does he realize that his garrison can scarcely outnumber my crew? La Belle Cerise carries one hundred and fifty-four as natty sailors as ever swung boarding-pikes, and at a pinch we can spare a round hundred for landing-party and still have enough on board to work our biggest guns. He should be thankful that I show an inclination to leave his puny fort untouched. What has he to say?"

"Our two nations being at war at the present time," announced the drummer, guardedly, "I am to tell you that we can offer no harbor unless you care to surrender yourself and crew as prisoners, and your ship as lawful prize. Failing this, you must—"

"What? Zounds!" howled the easily excited Frenchman. "Your Commandant may think this good jesting, but I do not share his opinions. Tell him to look to his defences. The flag of France shall once more wave above them. We will attack at once, and for every poor fellow I lose in this worthless assault, two of your survivors shall be strung up to die. Give way, my boys!" he cried, addressing his oarsmen.

The boat sped off to the vessel. The drummer and his little party returned within the fort, and prepared as best they could for what was to follow.

Almost immediately after the arrival of the privateer Captain on board his ship, three great pinnaces were lowered to the water and filled with men. The glitter from naked cutlasses, inlaid pistols, and carefully held muskets could easily be distinguished among them. This flotilla was soon ready, and at once started for the fort landing. Luckily for the trivial band of defenders the wind was increasing to such an extent that Captain Rabentine did not consider it wise to attempt manœuvring his ship in an unbuoyed and dangerous harbor. Therefore the flotilla was without any aid from the guns of La Belle Cerise. Moreover, the waves were commencing to run high, and the overloaded boats labored heavily. It was necessary to keep them headed to the seas as much as possible, and, in consequence, their progress towards the shore was rendered extremely slow.

Rupert Haydon and his improvised garrison were all ready. The loaded cannon were trained as nearly as could be upon the approaching boats. The women soldiers had kissed their children a fond good-bye, and shut them up in the bomb-proof magazine, away from danger of flying projectiles.

When the flotilla had arrived within easy range, the young drummer commenced discharging the battery as fast as he could pull the lanyards. After him hurried the women, reloading the heated cannon. The roar of the discharge came re-echoing back from the rocky cliffs repeated over and over again, and the smoke-clouds temporarily hid the fort from view.

This unskilful volley went wide of the mark, as was to be expected under the circumstances, and yet inflicted great damage upon the privateersmen. The thing came about after the following fashion: Upon the very beginning of the cannonade, the officer in command of the leading boat had bade his rowers swing their craft directly head on to the fort, thus presenting as small a target as possible. Those in the second boat, however, more intent upon watching the course of the projectiles than anything else, had not noticed this manœuvre, and so, before anything could be done to prevent it, came smashing against the other's gunwale. In the heavy sea then running this was specially disastrous. The stricken boat had her side stove in, and the on-comer was overturned. Both crews quickly found themselves struggling in the water. Well convinced of the hopelessness of continuing their present assault, the men in the remaining pinnace confined their efforts to rescuing drowning comrades and getting out of range again as quickly as possible.

The gale had now increased considerably, and its gathering force gave promise of still fiercer might. By the time the survivors of the boat expedition had returned to their ship the day was drawing close to twilight. Captain Rabentine well realized his double danger. Failing shelter, which could only be found farther up the harbor, and in range of the fort's cannon, he must put to sea. He was wild with anger at his repulse. What would have been his condition of mind if he had known that the defenders consisted merely of a boy and a few women dressed in soldier clothes?

Hastily ordering the cable slipped, Captain Rabentine saw to the spreading of some small storm-sails, and tried to beat out of the inhospitable harbor. But even here fortune seemed to be against him. The full flood-tide was running, and although La Belle Cerise strutted bravely, she could make no perceptible offing. The only road to safety lay directly past the fort and out the other entrance. The privateer Captain well knew that one lucky shot might disable his ship, and cause him to lose control over her. In such a wind and upon such a coast this meant almost certain death and destruction. But it appeared to be his only chance, and he had to take it.

Down on the wind swept the privateer. Her decks were awash with foam. She rolled and pitched like a mad thing. Her guns were lashed fast to the deck ring-bolts. It would have been suicidal to try to use them in such a sea. The crew clung to shrouds and railings, gazing ruefully upon the nearing battlements which they had so unsuccessfully attempted to assail. In a few minutes they were almost abreast of the green hill. Scarcely a hundred yards distant were the grinning embrasures, from which protruded the muzzles of cannon in plain view.

SHE ROLLED AND PITCHED LIKE A MAD THING

Within the fort Rupert Haydon stood ready, lanyard in hand. The guns had been more carefully sighted this time, and he felt sure that they could not all miss such a monstrous mark. One pull upon the blackened cord and the chances for a prosperous voyage of La Belle Cerise of St. Malo would be small. For a second he hesitated. Then dropping the lanyard, cried:

"No, no. It would be murder, not battle."

Seizing the white flag of truce that had already been used in the preliminary negotiations, and leaping upon the parapet, he waved it to and fro.

The meaning was instantly comprehended on board of the privateer. Not to be outdone in courtesy, some sailors, at risk of life and limb, scrambled aft to their own halyards. As the ship swept by, the proud ensign of France descended to the deck in salute to the drummer-boy of Warburton's. Ere it was hoisted again, La Belle Cerise was a receding speck upon the darkening, storm-swept ocean.

XV
ROGERS' RANGERS
THE FAMOUS NEW HAMPSHIRE SCOUTS OF THE OLD FRENCH WAR

Rogers' Rangers were a famous partisan corps during the old French War. Besides the regular forces employed, there were irregular or partisan bodies, composed of Canadian French and their Indian allies on one side, and English frontiersmen on the other. They acted as scouts and rangers for either army, guarding trains, procuring intelligence, and intercepting supplies destined for the enemy. Both were composed of picked men, skilled in woodcraft, and excellent marksmen. One of Rogers' companies was composed entirely of Indians in their native costume.

The Rangers were a body of hardy and resolute young men, principally from New Hampshire. They were accustomed to hunting and inured to hardships, and from frequent contact with the Indians they had become familiar with their language and customs. Every one of these rugged foresters was a dead shot, and could hit an object the size of a dollar at a hundred yards.

There was no idleness in the Rangers' camp. They were obliged to be constantly on the alert, and to keep a vigilant watch upon the enemy. They made long and fatiguing journeys into his country on snow-shoes in midwinter in pursuit of his marauding parties, often camping in the forest without a fire, to avoid discovery, and without other food than the game they had killed on the march. On more than one occasion they made prisoners of the French sentinels at the very gates of Crown Point and Ticonderoga, their strongholds. They were the most formidable body of men ever employed in Indian warfare, and were especially dreaded by their French and Indian foes.

It was in this school that Israel Putnam, John Stark, and others were trained for future usefulness in the struggle for American Independence. Several British officers, attracted by this exciting and hazardous as well as novel method of campaigning, joined as volunteers in some of their expeditions. Among them was the young Lord Howe, who during this tour of duty formed a strong friendship for Stark and Putnam, both of whom were with him when he fell at Ticonderoga shortly afterwards.

Major Robert Rogers, who raised and commanded this celebrated corps, was a native of Dunbarton, New Hampshire. Tall and well proportioned, but rough in feature, he was noted for strength and activity, and was the leader in athletic sports, not only in his own neighborhood, but for miles around.

Rogers' lieutenant was John Stark, afterwards the hero of Bennington. When in his twenty-fourth year Stark, while out with a hunting-party, was captured by some St. Francis Indians and taken to their village. While here he had to run the gauntlet. For this cruel sport the young warriors of the tribe arranged themselves in two lines, each armed with a rod or club to strike the captive as he passed them, singing some provoking words taught him for the occasion, intended to stimulate their wrath against the unfortunate victim.

Eastman, one of Stark's companions when he was taken, was the first to run the gauntlet and was terribly mauled. Stark's turn came next. Making a sudden rush, he knocked down the nearest Indian, and wresting his club from him, struck out right and left, dealing such vigorous blows as he ran that he made it extremely lively for the Indians, without receiving much injury himself. This feat greatly pleased the old Indians who were looking on, and they laughed heartily at the discomfiture of the young men.

When the Indians directed him to hoe corn, Stark cut up the young corn and flung his hoe into the river, declaring that it was the business of squaws and not of warriors. Stark was at length ransomed by his friends on payment of £100 to his captors.

During the Revolutionary war Stark's services were rendered at the most critical moments, and were of the highest value to his country. At Bunker Hill he commanded at the rail fence on the left of the redoubt, holding the post long enough to insure the safety of his overpowered and retreating countrymen. At the capture of the Hessians at Trenton he led the van of Sullivan's division, and at Bennington he struck the decisive blow that paralyzed Burgoyne and made his surrender inevitable.

Skilful and brave as were the Rangers, they were not always successful. The French partisans, under good leaders, with their wily and formidable Indian allies, well versed in forest strategy, on one occasion inflicted dire disaster upon them.

Near Fort Ticonderoga, in the winter of 1757, Rogers with 180 men attacked and dispersed a party of Indians, inflicting upon them a severe loss. This, however, was but a small part of the force which, under De la Durantaye and De Langry, French officers of reputation, were fully prepared to meet the Rangers, of whose movements they had been thoroughly informed beforehand. The party Rogers had dispersed was simply a decoy.

The Rangers had thrown down their packs, and were scattered in pursuit of the flying savages, when they suddenly found themselves confronted with the main body of the enemy, by whom they were largely outnumbered and of whose presence they were wholly unsuspicious. Nearly fifty of the Rangers fell at the first onslaught; the remainder retreated to a position in which they could make a stand. Here, under such cover as the trees and rocks afforded, they fought with their accustomed valor, and more than once drove back their numerous foes. Repeated attacks were made upon them both in front and on either flank, the enemy rallying after each repulse, and manifesting a courage and determination equal to those of the Rangers. So close was the conflict that the opposing parties were often intermingled, and in general were not more than twenty yards asunder. The fight was a series of duels, each combatant singling out a particular foe—a common practice in Indian fighting.

This unequal contest had continued an hour and a half, and the Rangers had lost more than half their number. After doing all that brave men could do, the remainder retreated in the best manner possible, each for himself. Several who were wounded or fatigued were taken by the pursuing savages. A singular circumstance about this battle was that it was fought by both sides upon snow-shoes.

Rogers, closely pursued, made his escape by outwitting the Indians who pressed upon him—such at least is the tradition. The precipitous cliffs near the northern end of Lake George, since called Rogers' Rock, has on one side a sharp and steep descent hundreds of feet to the lake. Gaining this point, Rogers threw his rifle and other equipments down the rocks. Then, unbuckling the straps of his snow-shoes, and turning round, he replaced them, the toes still pointing towards the lake. This was the work of a moment. He then walked back in his tracks from the edge of the cliff into the woods and disappeared just as the Indians, sure of their prey, reached the spot. To their amazement, they saw two tracks towards the cliff, none from it, and concluded that two Englishmen had thrown themselves down the precipice, preferring to be dashed to pieces rather than be captured. Soon a rapidly receding figure on the ice below attracted their notice, and the baffled savages, seeing that the redoubtable Ranger had safely effected the perilous descent, gave up the chase, fully believing him to be under the protection of the Great Spirit.

By a wonderful exercise of his athletic powers, Rogers, availing himself of the projecting branches of the trees which lined the rocky ravines in his course, had succeeded in swinging himself from the top to the bottom of this precipitous cliff. It was a fortunate escape for him, for if captured he would surely have been burned alive.

In this unfortunate affair the Rangers had eight officers and one hundred men killed. Their losses, however, were soon repaired, and they continued to render efficient service until the close of the war.

XVI
THE PLOT OF PONTIAC
HOW DETROIT WAS SAVED IN 1763

The long contest between England and France for the right to rule over North America, which lasted seventy years, and inflicted untold misery upon the hapless settlers on the English frontier, was at last brought to an end. England was victorious, and in 1763 a treaty was made by which France gave up Canada and all her Western posts.

With the exception of the Six Nations, the Indian tribes had fought on the side of the French, whose kind and generous course had won their affection. But the claims to the country which they and their forefathers had always possessed were utterly disregarded by both parties. Said an old chief on one occasion:

"The French claim all the land on one side of the Ohio, and the English claim all the land on the other side. Where, then, are the lands of the Indian?"

The final overthrow of the French left the Indians to contend alone with the English, who were steadily pushing them towards the setting sun. Seeing this, and wishing to rid his country of the hated pale-faces, who had driven the red men from their homes, Pontiac, the great leader of the Ottawas, determined—to use his own words—"to drive the dogs in red clothing" (the English soldiers) "into the sea."

This renowned warrior, who had led the Ottawas at the defeat of General Braddock, was courageous, intelligent, and eloquent, and was unmatched for craftiness. Besides the kindred tribes of Ojibways, or Chippewas, and Pottawattomies, whose villages were with his own in the immediate vicinity of Detroit, a number of other warlike tribes agreed to join in the plot to overthrow the English. Pontiac refused to believe that the French had given up the contest, and relied upon their assistance also for the success of his plan.

All the English forts and garrisons beyond the Alleghanies were to be destroyed on a given day, and the defenceless frontier settlements were also to be swept away.

The capture of Detroit was to be the task of Pontiac himself. This terrible plot came very near succeeding. Nine of the twelve military posts on the exposed frontier were taken, and most of their defenders slaughtered, and the outlying settlements of Pennsylvania and Virginia were mercilessly destroyed.

On the evening of May 6, 1763, Major Gladwin, the commander at Detroit, received secret information that an attempt would be made next day to capture the fort by treachery. The garrison was weak, the defences feeble. Fearing an immediate attack, the sentinels were doubled, and an anxious watch was kept by Gladwin all that night.

The next morning Pontiac entered the fort with sixty chosen warriors, each of whom had concealed beneath his blanket a gun, the barrel of which had been cut short. His plan was to demand that a council be held, and after delivering his speech to offer a peace belt of wampum. This belt was worked on one side with white and on the other side with green beads. The reversal of the belt from the white to the green side was to be the signal of attack. The plot was well laid, and would probably have succeeded had it not been revealed to Gladwin.

The savage throng, plumed and feathered and besmeared with paint to make themselves appear as hideous as possible, as their custom is in time of war, had no sooner passed the gateway than they saw that their plan had failed. Soldiers and employés were all armed and ready for action. Pontiac and his warriors, however, moved on, betraying no surprise, and entered the council-room, where Gladwin and his officers, all well armed, awaited them.

"Why," asked Pontiac, "do I see so many of my father's young men standing in the street with their guns?"

"To keep the young men to their duty, and prevent idleness," was the reply.

The business of the council then began. Pontiac's speech was bold and threatening. As the critical moment approached, and just as he was on the point of presenting the belt, and all was breathless expectation, Gladwin gave a signal. The drums at the door of the council suddenly rolled the charge, the clash of arms was heard, and the officers present drew their swords from their scabbards. Pontiac was brave, but this decisive proof that his plot was discovered completely disconcerted him. He delivered the belt in the usual manner, and without giving the expected signal.

Stepping forward, Gladwin then drew the chief's blanket aside, and disclosed the proof of his treachery. The council then broke up. The gates of the fort were again thrown open, and the baffled savages were permitted to depart.

Stratagem having failed, an open attack soon followed, but with no better success. For months Pontiac tried every method in his power to capture the fort, but as the hunting-season approached, the disheartened Indians gradually went away, and he was compelled to give up the attempt.

In the campaign that followed, two armies were marched from different points into the heart of the Indian country. Colonel Bradstreet, on the north, passed up the lakes, and penetrated the region beyond Detroit, while on the south Colonel Bouquet advanced from Fort Pitt into the Delaware and Shawnee settlements of the Ohio Valley. The Indians were completely overawed. Bouquet compelled them to sue for peace, and to restore all the captives that had been taken from time to time during their wars with the whites.

The return of these captives, many of whom were supposed to be dead, and the reunion of husbands and wives, parents and children, and brothers and sisters, presented a scene of thrilling interest. Some were overjoyed at regaining their lost ones; others were heartbroken on learning the sad fate of those dear to them. What a pang pierced that mother's breast who recognized her child only to find it clinging the more closely to its Indian mother, her own claims wholly forgotten!

Some of the children had lost all recollection of their former home, and screamed and resisted when handed over to their relatives. Some of the young women had married Indian husbands, and, with their children, were unwilling to return to the settlements. Indeed, several of them had become so strongly attached to their Indian homes and mode of life that after returning to their homes they made their escape and returned to their husbands' wigwams.

Even the Indians, who are educated to repress all outward signs of emotion, could not wholly conceal their sorrow at parting with their adopted relatives and friends. Cruel as the Indian is in his warfare, to his captives who have been adopted into his tribe he is uniformly kind, making no distinction between them and those of his own race. To those now restored they offered furs and choice articles of food, and even begged leave to follow the army home, that they might hunt for the captives, and supply them with better food than that furnished to the soldiers. Indian women filled the camp with their wailing and lamentation both night and day.

One old woman sought her daughter, who had been carried off nine years before. She discovered her, but the girl, who had almost forgotten her native tongue, did not recognize her, and the mother bitterly complained that the child she had so often sung to sleep had forgotten her in her old age.

Bouquet, whose humane instincts had been deeply touched by this scene, suggested an experiment. "Sing the song you used to sing to her when a child," said he. The mother sang. The girl's attention was instantly fixed. A flood of tears proclaimed the awakened memories, and the long-lost child was restored to the mother's arms.

THE END